where i want to be

where

i want

to be

ADELE GRIFFIN

G.P. PUTNAM'S SONS

NEW YORK

G. P. PUTNAM'S SONS
A division of Penguin Young Readers Group
Published by The Penguin Group
Penguin Group (USA) Inc., 375 Hudson Street, New York, NY 10014, U.S.A.

Penguin Group (Canada), 10 Alcorn Avenue, Toronto, Ontario, Canada M4V 3B2 •
(a division of Pearson Penguin Canada Inc.)
Penguin Books Ltd, 80 Strand, London WC2R 0RL, England.
Penguin Ireland, 25 St. Stephen's Green, Dublin 2, Ireland (a division of Penguin Books Ltd.)
Penguin Books India Pvt Ltd, 11 Community Centre, Panchsheel Park, New Delhi – 110 017, India.
Penguin Group (NZ), Cnr Airborne and Rosedale Roads, Albany, Auckland, New Zealand
(a division of Pearson New Zealand Ltd).
Penguin Books (South Africa) (Pty) Ltd, 24 Sturdee Avenue, Rosebank, Johannesburg 2196, South Africa.
Penguin Books Ltd, Registered Offices: 80 Strand, London WC2R 0RL, England.

Published simultaneously in Canada. Printed in the United States of America.
Design by Gunta Alexander. Text set in Nofret.

Library of Congress Cataloging-in-Publication Data
Griffin, Adele. Where I want to be / Adele Griffin. p. cm.
Summary: Two teenaged sisters, separated by death but still connected, work through their
feelings of loss over the closeness they shared as children that was later destroyed by one's
mental illness, and finally make peace with each other.
[1. Sisters–Fiction. 2. Mental illness–Fiction. 3. Death–Fiction. 4. Rhode Island–Fiction.] I. Title.
PZ7.G881325Wh 2005 [Fic]–dc22 2004001887 ISBN 0-399-23783-6
1 3 5 7 9 10 8 6 4 2
First Impression

where i want to be

Jane

"Augusta! Granpa!" Jane shouted. "I'm here!"

No lights lined the driveway.

The ancient maples blocked Jane's view of the house. She could hardly see a step ahead.

She started to run.

A soft wind hushed in her ears as she sprinted up the lawn. She smelled the verbena that grew in tangles on either side of the porch stairs. On her way up the steps, she lost her balance, stumbling against the front door and shifting the welcome mat so that the watermark showed underneath.

"Let me in!" She rapped the brass pineapple knocker, then made a fist and pounded the door. "It's Jane!"

The door opened. Light spilled onto the porch.

"Jane!" Her grandmother had grown up in North Carolina, and her accent pulled long on Jane's name. But she was not angry. She never was. Not even when Jane might have deserved it.

Like the time she'd smashed Augusta's crystal vase into a thousand needles all over the front hall.

Or when she let her grandparents' parakeet, Piccolo, out of his cage and watched him fly away into the woods, never to return.

Or when she'd taken a paring knife from the kitchen rack and stabbed it through the soft skin between her thumb and finger. Just to change something. Just to feel something.

Even then, stanching the blood with a clean dishcloth, her grandmother had looked maybe shocked, maybe fierce. But not angry.

Never angry.

It might have been the thing Jane loved most about her.

"I didn't know where else to go . . ." Jane stopped. She had been alone for so long, stretched across the blackness, terrified that she would not find Orchard Way at the end of this journey. Now here she was, at the only place where she'd always belonged.

She sagged into the door frame. She was out of breath and strength. "I need to rest," she admitted.

Augusta pulled her close. Jane shut her eyes and let herself be hugged, although hugs made her queasy. But it had been more than two years since she had seen her grandmother. The familiar smells wrapped themselves around her. Augusta's lavender hand cream, the pine soap in the floorboards, the mushroomy dampness and smoke in the wallpaper. Tears prickled at the edges of Jane's eyelids as she gently pushed her grandmother away. Hadn't she been upset with Augusta for something?

The reason escaped her. It didn't matter. She was through with reasons, and she was home.

Lily

Jane died this past spring, but we can't talk about it. In fact, we kind of give up on talking. It's not some kind of eloquent, dramatic decision. It just happens. An eighteen-year-old girl crosses a two-way street on a changing light. A moving car hits and kills her instantly. The Metro section of the paper reports that services for Jane Ellen Calvert will be held on Saturday morning at St. Thomas, and to please make a donation to Child Haven in place of flowers.

She's gone. What else is there to say?

We use work to cope, or maybe to hide. The college grants Dad's request to teach a summer chemistry course. Mom goes back to selling houses for Payne-Hazard Realty. I start my job at Small Farms. We meet at home for dinner. Sometimes Caleb joins us.

It's strange how so much life can be lived without speaking. By the end of summer, the silence has grown up as thick as weeds around our days. But at unexpected moments, I can feel Jane with me. Silence can't keep her away. She might be here when I'm stuck in traffic, or eating a sandwich, or brushing my hair. Or she's inside my sleep, in a waking dream where I kick the sheets and feel sweat stick cold under my arms and at the backs of my knees. Memories of every time I ever hurt Jane swoop like bats in my brain. I am a monster. I hate myself.

At the end of August, Mom and Dad decide to take a weeklong trip to Maine to visit Aunt Gwen and Uncle Dean. They invite me along, but I can't go.

"You won't be too lonely?"

"I'd feel worse without Caleb."

Dad doesn't like that. He isn't the kind of dad who wants to discuss guys or romance. He's proper, I guess. A mix of Granpa's Yankee reserve and Augusta's Southern gentility. "Look out for Mr. Wild and Crazy," Mom will tease if Dad pours himself a second glass of wine or retells a joke he heard in the faculty room.

When it comes to Caleb, Dad is not Mr. Wild and Crazy as much as Mr. Frowning and Protective. But that's just Dad. He'll never be totally at ease with my boyfriends—in concept or reality. For the most part, though, both of my parents are cool about Caleb. They know what Caleb means to me.

And they agree to let me stay at the house by myself. Jane never would have been given this privilege.

"You're almost seventeen," Mom assures herself, doing a

final contents-of-pocketbook check as Dad hauls their suit-cases out to the car. "You're responsible." Her cucumber green shirt clashes with her hair. She's just started tinting it to cover the gray that's been creeping in. Mom has–and passed down–what Jane once called our spicy coloring. Cinnamon red hair and nutmeg brown eyes and skin cayenne-peppered with freckles. But Jane had a way of de-scribing things so that they seemed better or worse than they really are. Other people would just call us redheads.

There's a pinch between Mom's eyebrows as she looks at me.

"Mom, I'll be fine."

She doesn't look convinced. "You'll check on Mrs. Orn-dorff? And you'll set the alarms at night?"

"Yes, yes."

"You have enough gas in the car?"

"Filled the tank yesterday."

"If you change your mind, you'll just hop the next train? It's less than four hours from Providence. We'll keep our phones on. Just let us know when you need us to pick you up." Mom bites her bottom lip and her whole body seems to soften from the pressure. "Oh, honestly, Lily. You've been working hard all summer. You could use some time off be-fore school starts. You can swim in the lake. . . ." Her fingers are like rubber bands as she snaps them around my wrist. The urgency in her eyes reminds me of my sister. "I worry about you sleeping alone here."

"Mom, please. I've slept here my whole life."

"But never alone."

True. But I have no intention of sleeping alone. Not if I've got Caleb. Some part of Mom has to have figured that one out by now. She's not clueless. Or maybe this is why she's letting me stay? Because she knows that Caleb and I have each other?

After I hug them both and wave good-bye, I make a bowl of cereal and watch the news on TV. Then I eat an Italian ice and read one of Mom's gardening magazines. Then I pour a glass of iced tea and sit on the patio stoop and stare at the sunset.

Once it gets dark, I pad through the house. Inspecting it. From the outside, 47 Clearview Circle is nothing much, one of a dozen white-painted, black-shuttered, single-story homes set on a quarter acre. It's the trees that make our house special. The ming fern, the twin red Japanese maples, the towering buttonwood—once the site of Peace Dale's coolest tree house. Mom's trees are the pride of the neighborhood, like movie stars who've shown up at a backyard barbecue.

Inside, our house looks shabby. Mom and Dad will save for college funds or retirement funds or rainy-day funds, but never for something as wasteful as a redecorating fund. Everywhere, I see thumbprints of Jane. Here's the butterfly-shaped stain on the carpet where Jane spilled cranberry juice. On the wall, a picture hanger minus its picture of

Block Island harbor that Jane had made for our parents' fifteenth wedding anniversary, but then yanked down and ripped up because of the "stupid amateur mistakes."

My own bedroom tries too hard to be cheerful. Rainbow pillows are heaped on my polka-dot bedspread, and daisy-chain lights are strung along the windows. A watercolor poster from Peace Dale's Hot Air Balloon Festival is tacked to my door. But my room is Jane damaged, too. Not from what's there, but from what's missing. Like books Jane "borrowed" out of my bookshelf and clothes on loan from my closet. Or the empty corner that held my green frog beanbag chair, thrown out after Jane plunged through it with a pair of garden shears.

I walk to the end of the hall and open the door to Jane's room. As soon as I switch on the light, I see something new. A pile of freshly folded clothes rests on Jane's bed. As if any minute she'll come bounding in to put them away. Must have been Mom. Dad shares laundry duty, but only Mom would cling to the hope that Jane might come back.

Most of Jane's belongings are secondhand. Mom's old stuffed-animal horses, Rags and Patches, slump side by side on her dusty dresser. Dad's desktop model of the solar system is also fluffed with dust, and so is the seat on Granpa's rocking chair that my grandmother gave Jane after he died. Jane liked to surround herself with other people's things. They comforted her, I guess, when people themselves could not.

I snap off the light and the fuse blows, and I scream softly as my fingers zap. That's when I feel it again. It grips me, like two hands squeezing me around the waist, cutting off the air from my diaphragm and knocking me from my feet. I sit at the foot of Jane's bed, my arms cradled at my middle, working to breathe.

"Jane?" I speak her name into the dark. The room holds the word.

All through that morning, throughout the plump-cheeked minister's sermon about shy, gentle Jane, I'd wanted to laugh. Shy Jane? Gentle Jane? *Selfish, wild, thoughtless, brave*—I'd start with those words, but even they aren't right.

I worry that I'm already forgetting pieces of her.

"Jane," I say, louder, "you'd laugh to see your room like this, so clean. I'll mess it up a little, if you want. Just give me the signal."

I sound like an idiot. I know I do. But I jump up from her bed and tug the wrinkles from her bedspread. Then I force myself to leave Jane's room. Careful to shut the door on my way out.

Jane

In the kitchen, Jane ate her special foods. Her grandfather shuffled back and forth from the counter to the table. He heaped her plate.

"All your favorites."

Jane clapped her hands. A banquet. Buttered, warm rolls. Sliced ruby tomatoes. Perfect spheres of vanilla ice cream. Cantaloupe. Pale, cold milk. Pinks and whites and reds, too good to be true, and Jane knew that it wasn't true. Not exactly. The food was here because she needed it to be here. The rules were different now. Now everything was as real as she made it.

Even her happiness felt too good. Like she'd borrowed it from somebody else.

And she knew that she was too old to eat with her fingers, but Augusta let her. Then she let Jane spoon-scrape melted ice cream from the bottom of her dish.

"I'm going to stay with you forever." She used to say this a lot when she was younger. "I'll sleep in Dad's old room. I'll watch movies and eat ice cream. I don't need anything else. I never did."

Augusta had Choctaw Indian in her blood, which gave her bones their sensible shape. She had looked the same for as long as Jane could remember. Tall and heavyset, a rugged tree of a grandmother who wove her hair into a silver cable down her back and dressed in pastel pants and denim shirts, or vice versa.

"Let's get you to bed," she said. "I'll lend you one of my nightshirts."

"I'll wash up here," said Granpa.

Her father's room was off the second-floor landing. Part of his childhood was left behind here. A prism decal shimmered in the window, and a paint-chipped bookshelf was filled with weary hardcovers about Galileo and Einstein and Crick. As a boy, her father had loved science, and he still did. He was a chemistry professor at Providence Community College, where students called him Ray instead of Dr. Calvert and dedicated the yearbook to him an average of once every three and a half years.

When she was younger, Jane used to imagine that her father's room belonged to her instead. "Let's pretend," she'd coax Lily. "Pretend I'm Granpa and Augusta's daughter instead of their granddaughter. Pretend that you're visiting me and it's olden days from when Dad was little. You start. Say, 'Hi, Aunt Jane!' Then ask my permission to unpack your suitcase."

"But you're not my aunt! We're *sisters*," Lily would wail. "One hundred percent *sisters*. I *hate* your stupid pretending away of the truth! And I hate olden days!"

"If you can't pretend to be in other times and places, you'll be stuck in the real world forever," Jane would warn. "And the real world isn't half as good."

But Lily seemed to get along just fine in the real world.

Her grandparents were different. They liked olden days. Granpa knew the whole history of Peace Dale. Before he'd retired, he'd worked at the Rhode Island Historical Center. It was Granpa who showed Jane the home of Mary Butterworth, the sneaky counterfeiter who bought a mansion in Providence with money she'd made herself, using a quill pen and copperplates. Granpa who showed Jane the Old Stone Mill that had been built a thousand years ago by Norse Vikings.

Augusta was not much for field trips or stories. But her presence was like a lullaby.

"Don't go yet," Jane said now, reaching out her hand.

Augusta did not leave. She stayed at the edge of the bed and skimmed her fingertips up and down the length of Jane's arm. The sheets were as crisp as a tablecloth against Jane's skin, and the sink of the mattress molded to the shape of her body. She closed her eyes and pulled the edge of the linsey-woolsey blanket so that it brushed her chin. A linsey-woolsey blanket was folded at the edge of every bed at Orchard Way. They were famous blankets, knit by Peace Dale's own textile mills and dyed with walnut shells to mossy greens and browns. During the Civil War, thousands of these blankets had been distributed to Union soldiers.

"Pretend I'm a soldier," Jane used to suggest to Lily, "and I'm about to die from frostbite on the battlefield, and you're a poor factory girl named Hepsbeth, and you find me and cover me with a blanket just in time."

Lily had liked that game better. Lily liked to rescue people.

"How long can I stay?" Jane asked Augusta sleepily.

"Until you want to go." Her grandmother's voice sounded far away.

Yes, that was a nice answer. Sleep was falling softly over her. "Orchard Way is my only place," she mumbled. She burrowed deeper, darker, safer.

Her grandmother didn't answer, but her fingers continued to trace the length of Jane's arm. Up and down, up and down. She would not stop until Jane was asleep.

Lily

Caleb drops by late. After his own day at the Pool & Paddle Youth Club, he had to work a shift at the Co-op for a friend. But he bangs through the door with his dimpled smile locked in place. His guitar is in one hand, and a bag of something that smells yummy is in the other.

"You could have called," I say, wrapping my arms around his neck. My lips touch his throat, his chin, and the tip of his nose. "I'da picked you up. I hate thinking of you walking all this way."

"The fastest journey is achieved on foot," Caleb answers grandly. Thoreau, most likely. Caleb is something of a Thoreau fiend. He lets me reclaim him a few seconds longer. Then he shakes the bag. "You eaten?"

"No." The cereal was hours ago. I'm hungry again.

We set up for a nighttime feast at the picnic table out back. I even light the tea candles and get out the coasters, self-consciously adult without Mom and Dad around. We

talk about next month and the start of my senior year at
North Peace Dale High. I've gotten expert at dodging
around the subject of what Caleb is planning to do this
fall. My standing policy on that is to wait for him to bring
it up.

Instead, I ask him what happened today at the Pool &
Paddle, where Caleb teaches swimming. It's the right job
for him, mixing his love of kids with his near-perfect pa-
tience.

"Nothing much. Actually, one of my tadpoles drew me a
picture."

"Oh, cute! Do you have it? Let me see!"

Sheepish, Caleb pulls it from his wallet, unfolding it with
care, and passes it over. But he knows I'll like it.

The picture is of two stick figures. Same height, squiggly
spider hands joined and wearing shoes that look like flow-
erpots. Behind them is a blue blob, which I guess is the
pool.

For Coach Caleb love Sophie marches in painstaking print
across the bottom.

"Those kids love you. You have such a good heart," I tell
him.

"Yeah, yeah, yeah," he answers. He's shy about compli-
ments.

"Seriously." I tweak the pink tip of his ear.

"Hey, you're the one who bakes chocolate chip cookies
for crazy old ladies."

"Mrs. Orndorff's not crazy, she's a sweetie pie. Especially if you make her cookies."

"Which reminds me." Caleb reaches up and swipes a couple of plates off the top shelf just as the toaster oven timer pings. "I'm starved."

After more than a year of semi-conversion to Caleb's vegan diet, soy cheese still tastes like soggy paper to me, but it doesn't stop me from polishing off two veggie burritos. Then I dig out the last lemon Italian ice in the freezer for dessert. We move off the picnic bench to sit on the stoop, sharing a spoon, scraping and passing the carton back and forth as we check out the stars.

"Lesson?" Caleb suggests.

"Okay, but, warning—I don't think I've improved since last time."

"How about just as an excuse to sit close to you and breathe down your neck?"

"Oh, well, sure. In that case."

He stuffs stray burrito wrappings and napkins back into the paper sack, and then places the guitar across my lap and swings a leg around so that he's sitting behind me. I'm not exactly passionate about these guitar lessons. I've got hypersensitive, redhead's skin, and the strings always feel like they're about to draw blood from my fingertips. But nothing feels sexier than Caleb sitting so close, the insides of his thighs hard against the outsides of my thighs, his fingers pressing over mine, his breath in my ear as he explains frets and chord progression. Always breath-minty breath, too, because Caleb is totally paranoid about halitosis.

We strum through some chords. Caleb's talented. He learned guitar from his uncle Rory, a burned-out music genius who lives in Venice Beach. Unfortunately, I'm no Uncle Rory. After I mangle an old Eric Clapton song, the pads of my fingers begin to welt.

"End of lesson," I tell him.

"A'right, ma'am, then I'll have to demand some payment."

The only thing sexier than Caleb sitting behind me is when he leans forward to kiss me. Warm, mint mouth, palms cupping the edge of my face. So slow, as if he is living only inside right now, without a hungry eye on what might come next. For a second, though, I think I sense something different, a funny-shaped moment where Cay seems to almost-but-maybe-not shift away from me.

"Something wrong?"

"Just . . . these damn mosquitoes," Caleb says.

"What are you talking about? There's no mosquitoes. It hasn't rained for weeks."

In response, he makes a halfhearted slap at the side of his neck.

I pull away. "Caleb, if you don't want to fool around, you don't need to invent some pathetic lie about it."

"I'm not . . ." He slaps his forearm, too deep in.

Now I'm annoyed, so I stand up in a huff and head inside. I scoop up the remote and turn on the television. Caleb, following me, flops onto the couch and yawns.

"Okay. The thing is . . . Mike Heller's having a party at his place." Caleb forces the casual tone in his voice. "Tonight."

"Eh," I answer. I press the channel changer.

Caleb clears his throat. "I've been thinking. We've been us two pretty much every night. I dunno, Lily. It might be good to get out. See kids."

"We see kids every day at work."

"You know what I mean, smart-ass. Our-age kids. Even if we don't want to . . ."

I turn from the screen. Caleb scratches at the late-night fuzz that shades his jawline. I won't say what I'm feeling. This summer, I'm too old for fun and parties.

"Next party," I say. "Next time. Promise. Just, not tonight."

"Right." He seems disappointed. I act like I don't notice.

"Besides, this is fun, isn't it?" I wish I could sound a little more joyful about it. "Playing house? No 'rents?"

"Mmm."

The truth is, it's not that different from when Mom and Dad are home, cloistered in their bedroom to watch their own TV and give us some privacy.

I shinny down on the couch next to him and stretch out on my side. Our bodies curve together. Familiar, but not so relaxed that there isn't a charge there. Or at least, I feel the charge, even though it's been one year, nine months, three weeks, and five days since Caleb and I started seeing each other. It doesn't seem like real time, though. It feels like one single, perfect day blended with forever. But our two-year anniversary is real enough. October 10.

We doze through a horror movie. My head is propped on a cushion that rests on Caleb's shoulder. My fingers drag lightly up and down his forearm, the way my grandmother used to do when I was a kid to get me to sleep. Caleb's arm is as thin as mine, chlorine bleached and nearly hairless.

"Something happened to me today," he says. "At the pool."

There's a quiet flutter in my blood. "What?"

"I wasn't going to tell you, but . . ."

"Tell me."

Now Caleb speaks in a rush, like he's been holding it in all evening. "It was during kick practice. I had the five through eights. My kids are all lined up with their paddle-boards in the shallow end, and I'm standing in front of them, I'm yelling *Kick! Kick!*, the water's churning, and I've got this whole line of noisy little squirts kicking like crazy." He pauses to smile. He loves his job. "All I was thinking about was making sure nobody kicked too close or hard—no fighting, no biting. And then."

"And then?"

He clears his throat. "You know that kinda prickly thing that happens on your skin if someone's staring at you from behind? It was like that. But stronger. Only when I turned to look? Nobody. All day I'm trying to think how to describe it, but the best I came up with is it felt like a piece of cobweb or something had landed right . . . here." He reaches around to the small of his back. "Except as soon as it happened, I thought—no, I *knew*." Caleb corrects himself.

"Knew . . . ?" My fingertips still hurt. I press them against my neck.

"Look, I'm not saying Jane was watching me for real." Caleb darts me an uneasy look. "It's more like she was there because she's in my head. She's . . . I dunno. *Around*." He swipes a hand back through his hair. "Ah, just tell me to shut up. Hearing myself talk about it, it sounds totally insane."

"No, it doesn't." I shake my head. "So, what did you do? At the pool, I mean."

"Got out. Cooled off. Let Maureen take over for a few minutes."

Caleb is being serious, but I'm not really sure what it is that he's told me, so I'm not really sure how to respond. "I was in Jane's bedroom earlier tonight," I confide, "and I had the same feeling. I think. Caleb . . ." I slide up on an elbow to look at him. "Do you ever feel guilty?"

This is exactly the kind of question Caleb hates. Something close to panic holds his eyes; one a bleached blue, the other a dark, marbled navy. Odd, definitely, but I think they're amazing. Even if the whites are bloodshot from pool chlorine and his chronic lack of sleep.

"The thing you can't forget in all this . . ." He stops. I wait him out. "What you can't forget, is that you weren't re-sponsible for how Jane was."

"You say that, but I know I could have helped her bet-ter. Somehow."

Caleb shakes his head. "We've had this talk a zillion times, Lily. There was no way for you to have known. You keep beating yourself up for not noticing, for not seeing the changes. But nobody else saw them, either. Why do you put all the blame on yourself?" His confidence envelops me, al-most.

"Because I'm her sister," I answer, "and I should have been able to do more. For all I know, I was part of the problem. Maybe we both were." With this last sentence, my voice is so low, I can hardly hear myself.

But Caleb hears me fine. He looks angry. "How were we the problem? Just by existing? By being us?"

"By being happy." I know I'm on shaky logic ground here. "Maybe it made us selfish. It must have hurt her."

Caleb's bony shoulder flinches in defense. "Being happy isn't our fault."

"Okay." I make my voice dull, agreeing and not agreeing. Our zillion-and-oneth talk is not going anywhere. I drop it. Lean back against him and try to anesthetize myself with TV. I imagine kids arriving at Mike Heller's house. Mike's a senior, and I picture his party crowded with other seniors–Jane's classmates, although I'm better friends with most of them, mostly on account of dating Caleb.

Heller's would be a total scene. First kids would make this whole big joyfest of seeing me, *oh, hey, wow, glad you made it, great to see ya,* and then there'd be the usual gossiping behind their hands, scrutinizing me, passing judgments about how I'm doing *really.* And I just do not want to deal with it.

"Stay here with me tonight, Cay?" It's a plea, but I try to make it sound like a suggestion. I move to tuck my arm underneath Caleb's waist. So thin, not a scrap more flesh on him than necessary. Wrapping myself closer, I whisper, "You make me feel so safe."

One of Caleb's scarecrow legs hooks and twines through mine. This means he'll stay and keep me safe the way I need him to. But I also can feel myself holding on too hard, relying on him too much. *Be with me, stay with me, don't leave me.* As if I've lost my hold on the world around me, and he's the only grip I've got.

Jane

Jane woke up yelling. In her mouth, in her open eyes, the darkness poured into her.

She sat up in bed and remembered. She was safe. She was at her grandparents' house. And she had not been yelling. Not out loud, anyway.

Thunder rumbled. That must have been the sound that woke her. Rain was driving hard on the rooftop and against the window. She slipped from the bed and out of the bedroom. Every floorboard, every piece of furniture at Orchard Way was so familiar to her that her imagination could shape whatever her sight couldn't reach. But she kept a hand on the banister as she tiptoed down the stairs, touching each step as lightly as a dancer.

Years ago, she and Lily used to play a game called Squeak. The winner was the one who could make it all the way up and back down the stairs the quietest. Only Jane got too good at it. She'd learned the mystery of each step, just as she'd learned every other secret thing about her grandparents' house.

When Lily stopped coming regularly to Orchard Way, Jane continued to play the game alone. Winning over and over against an invisible Lily.

At the front door, Jane turned the knob and stepped out onto the porch. The rain echoed on the roof, as loud as charging hooves. Could Lily hear it, too? Lily always used to wake up in storms. They'd terrified her, sent her flying into Jane's room, where she'd fling herself into Jane's bed and shiver under the covers. But storms at Orchard Way were beautiful and startling. Jane refused to let Lily hide through them. Instead, she'd coax her outside to play Run-away Horse.

"Pretend you're Finnegan, a wild stallion," Jane would say, "and pretend I'm Señor Jorge, the horse catcher who is coming to tame you for the circus!"

Once she had turned into a horse, Lily would forget about being afraid. Together, she and Jane would race through the slopping wet grass, raindrops smacking their arms and legs, Jane tugging the reins of Lily's hair and yelling, "There is no escape for you, Finn!" as Lily screeched in terror and delight.

Settled on the ladder-back rocker, Jane let it tilt her back and forth, back and forth. Finnegan and Señor Jorge! They had seemed so real back then. When Jane thought back on some of those old pretending games, they seemed so strange. As if somebody else had thought them up. As if they weren't from her mind at all.

She had missed being here. Missed it dull like a sickness and missed it sharp as a thousand scratches on her heart. Orchard Way had been the perfect place for snowstorms and thunderstorms and swimming and fort building, for birthdays and weekends and games and more games. It was a house of pretending impossible things. It was her whole, entire childhood blended into one single, perfect day that she thought would never end.

Back and forth. The rocker creaked if Jane pressed too hard against its spine. She tilted and held it with the tips of her toes as she watched another break of lightning, followed by a boom of thunder so loud that now she knew. Lily was awake.

Lily

The thunder wakes me up. It takes me a minute to remember where I am, on the couch, with my arms and legs pretzel-twisted around Caleb.

Through the living room window, I can see the summer storm raging. It's a biggie, electric with lightning. I untangle myself from Caleb's limbs and ease myself to my feet to double-check that all the windows are closed. *Not scared not scared*, I chant as I pad through the house. *Lalala*. Storms are definitely in my top five list of things that petrify me.

Kitchen, living room. The patio door is closed, but–oops–I'd left it unlocked. Parents' room, my room. At the end of the hall, the door to Jane's room, I hesitate.

Then I take a breath and turn the knob.

Her window is wide open. Rain blows in slantways, rattling the blinds up and down like a xylophone. My throat catches in senseless panic as I rush toward it. I can feel the carpet soaked and spongy under my feet. I lean up, struggling, but the window is stuck fast. Water sops my T-shirt and beats against my face. "C'mon, c'mon."

The window gives so suddenly that it almost takes off my fingers as it slams shut. Quickly, I turn the latch and step back, wiping the spray from my face.

The rocking chair is wet. It creaks back and forth as if by an invisible hand. I pluck a cotton T-shirt from the stack on Jane's bed and use it to dry the wood. The skin of my fingers stings where it tore. My heart is still thumping. I sit on the chair to calm myself. The rocking motion soothes me. I tilt myself into the rhythm as I listen to the rain.

When I was little, I used to head straight for Jane's room whenever I heard thunder. She was totally unafraid of it. Her brave face made me feel brave, too.

"Don't worry, Lily," she'd comfort me. "Storms are only angels having temper tantrums." Then she'd tickle her finger up and down the length of my arm, like Augusta did, to help me sleep. "See? It's a magic trick," she told me. "It hypnotizes you." I wasn't sure if that was true, but magic seemed to live in Jane's skin, as much a part of her as the games she would invent for us to play.

Like Spying on the Hobhouses, where we eavesdropped on an imaginary family who lived in Granpa's barn. Or Getting the Gold, where Jane would bury a sandwich bag full of loose change, and then present me with a map that would have me digging all day to find it. Or Wherever It Takes You, which was nothing more than following a bumblebee into the garden or woods, but mostly into trouble if we wandered off too far.

I'd happily play along with any of Jane's games back then. Jane enchanted my world. I thought my sister could do anything.

Realizing that she couldn't must have come on gradually, but I always pin it to one day. We'd been snapping string beans at the kitchen table at our grandparents' house, which Jane had named Orchard Way. Jane loved renaming things, but "Orchard Way" was wrong. Too snooty for a small house plopped on a patch of Peace Dale farmland.

I'd taken off my new bracelet, which was actually a bendable pencil, glittery pink. I was proud of it, and I could feel Jane stealing jealous glances.

"Where'd you get that?" she asked me finally.

"From the goody bag at Josie Hull's birthday party." Josie Hull was in Jane's class, but I'd been the one invited to Josie's tenth birthday party since we played league soccer together. Jane did not play soccer. She didn't play any sports at all.

"Granpa and Augusta'd get me one of those pencil bracelets if I wanted," Jane said after a minute. "All I'd have to do is ask."

"They would not."

"Would. They love me. Actually, more than they love you."

"Lie," I answered automatically. Then, "How do you know? Did they tell you that?"

"Not in words." Jane snapped a bean in half and checked it for spots. "But you can see from how they treat me."

It was true that our grandparents seemed to prefer Jane. They let her ramble on about her dreams, and they laughed at her unfunniest jokes. It had never really bothered me. After all, I had everything else, and I was slowly becoming more aware of that. Better looks and better grades and more friends. I had plenty. I had too much.

But if my grandparents actually loved my sister more, well, that seemed just about illegal. I wasn't a bad granddaughter. I said please, and I scraped my plate and put it in the dishwasher without being asked, and I never threw a Jane-style temper tantrum that swept through the house like a typhoon and bent everyone to its will.

"Why? Why do they love you more?" I'd asked her bravely.

"You know why." Jane's eyes fixed on me. "Because I have Special Needs. That's why Mom takes me to Dr. Beigeleisen every Thursday after school, but not you. Because of my Special Needs."

I simmered. Jane made it sound so good, but I knew the truth. Jane's Special Needs were nothing to brag about. As Mom had explained it, Special Needs meant extra help for Jane's tantrums and bad moods. But I knew that Special Needs also put the worry in Mom's and Dad's forehead.

Special Needs was a problem. It was no reason to get extra love. No way.

"After Mom and I drop you off at Dr. Beigeleisen's," I said, "we go to Newport Creamery and get Awful Awfuls, with real whipped cream. Maybe Augusta and Granpa love you more, but Mom loves me the *most.*"

Mom had sworn me not to tell about the Awful Awfuls. The clench in my stomach confirmed that I'd done something bad.

In that second, though, it was worth it. Just to see the horror pop the smugness off Jane's face.

"Liar," she whispered.

I said nothing. I snapped another bean and stuck out my tongue.

She pushed up from the table and slammed outside. I heard her calling to our grandparents' mutt, Gambler. Who also loved her best.

I snapped the rest of the beans by myself, although the job was too big for just me. But I was scared to ask a grown-up for help. Jane shouldn't have told me that our grandparents loved her best, but somehow I knew I'd done worse.

That day marked the beginning. Not because it was our first big fight, but because it was the first time I realized that I could hurt my sister if I chose. She might be half magic, but she was also half glass. It scared her to be shut out of my world of pink glitter bracelets and sleepovers and streams of friends and, later, Caleb. And I didn't mean to shut her out, but sometimes I did it anyway. I liked having power. Power is its own kind of magic.

The rocker squeaks me back and forth, lulling me to sleep. I imagine that Jane is with me again. In the next moment, knowing that she isn't, that she never will be, seems almost too much to bear.

In a determined push, I bounce to my feet and stretch. Then I leave Jane's room for the second time in one night. Heading back to the couch, back to Caleb's warm body, and the comfort of his skinny arms.

Jane

Morning sunshine warmed the breeze through the window curtains. Last night's rain had made the world damply fresh.

Jane flipped back the covers and smiled.

Outside, she heard Granpa whistle to Gambler, who was barking at something. The harder Jane listened, the more she was sure that Gambler was speaking to her.

"Jane! Get going!" he barked. "Jane! Put on your bathing suit and join us!"

But dogs didn't talk, Jane reminded herself. Gambler could speak only because she wasn't taking her medication. Her meds had kept her planted in a world where dogs barked and birds sang and yesterday seemed connected logically to today and tomorrow.

This morning, even without the pills, she felt all right. She felt free.

In a perfect world, a dog could talk, and it wasn't such a bad thing after all.

"Jane! Hurry!" barked Gambler. "Sleepyhead!"

On the closet door hook, Jane reclaimed her favorite bathing suit. It was a red-checkered one-piece, an old favorite that she thought she'd lost forever but now once again fit perfectly. In the mirror she saw herself. Flat edged and lanky. Like in her ballerina years, before she'd been padded down into a body that she'd never gotten the hang of.

She could not feel any of that chunky softness now.

"I'm the right shape again," she said to her reflection. "I'm me again."

She danced down the stairs and through the dining room. She spun in perfect pirouettes. Once her parents had taken her and Lily to Boston to see *The Nutcracker*. Sitting upright and trembling from her seat in the audience, Jane had watched Klara swoop across the stage in her lace nightgown and pink slippers. White-hot footlights were mirrored in her eyes, and her muscles flexed with every leap and turn. Jane could sense it all exactly. It took nothing for her imagination to spin it all into memory.

"Why are you telling kids you were in *The Nutcracker* ballet?" Lily had confronted her a week later.

"Because . . . " Jane faltered. Hadn't she been?

"Kids think you're the biggest liar in the school. They say you lie about tons of things."

"No, I don't."

But Jane saw the suspicion in Lily's face, and the shame.

It wasn't true, then? She hadn't danced in *The Nutcracker*? Not for real? Not just a little bit?

Because the difference was important. For Lily, *for real* was like a green light and *not for real* was a red light. Opposite colors that blinked separately and did not interfere with each other. But somehow, Jane seemed to see only one color. And sometimes that color shone very, very brightly.

Now Jane leaped in her best imitation of Klara. She jolted against the china cupboard, rattling Augusta's prized collection of handmade Mexican plates.

In a perfect world, nothing fell, and nothing broke.

She danced into the kitchen. It was empty. Her grandparents must be down by the pool. She took a plate from the cupboard. Five round scoops of cantaloupe for the mouth. Two pads of butter for eyes. A toasted roll nose. She smiled back at her smiley-face breakfast, tucked a napkin through the strap of her bathing suit, and trotted outside.

Swallowtail butterflies and yellow jackets swooped and dropped in the air. Augusta's impatiens was sprayed with purple and white blooms, but the azalea bushes were crumbly brown and the hydrangeas looked parched.

Her grandparents were lounging in lawn chairs. The green-striped table umbrella was cranked up. Augusta was filling in her morning crossword puzzle. Granpa's tackle box was open in front of him. He was rethreading his baits.

"Good morning," sang Augusta.

Granpa patted the chair between them. "So we can share you."

Jane set her plate down next to the tackle box.

"Well, look at that. You made a face." Augusta nodded approvingly. "That's as pretty as something in a restaurant. Such a talent with crafts, Jane."

Jane smiled back. She stretched her legs. Her toes brushed against Gambler, who was collapsed under the table between them. She dropped him a piece of her roll.

"Delicious, thanks," he panted. Then he rolled on his back for a stomach rub. Obligingly, Jane nudged her toes over his tummy.

With Jane at the table, Augusta didn't seem much interested in her puzzle anymore.

"Sleep well?"

"I woke up from the thunder."

Granpa was listening, too. It had never been hard for Jane to hold her grandparents' interest. Their eyes were shiny on her. Their smiles wanted more.

"And then I dreamed I was a rock climber," Jane told them now.

"A rock climber? Oh, you do beat all," drawled Augusta.

"Tell us," said Granpa.

So Jane told them her dream, taking her time and adding details. Her grandparents were her best dream listeners.

She swallowed her cantaloupe and used her fingers to

spread the butter on her roll. After she finished eating, she lolled back in her chair. Her mouth and hands were hot, buttery, sticky. She could eat melon and buttered rolls every single day and never be tired of them.

And she didn't need to say this to her grandparents, because they already knew.

"Maybe I'll water the plants," she said. "They look thirsty."

"Why, that's a good idea," said Augusta.

"The sprinkling can's under the porch," added Granpa.

Yes, she'd water the plants. Maybe weed out the dandelions. And then she'd skim the leaves out of the pool after rescuing any stray daddy longlegs from the surface. Summer had always been Jane's favorite time at Orchard Way. Lazy days, but with the most odd jobs.

Lily never treasured Sundays like Jane did. By the time she was in sixth grade, Lily was making other weekend plans. Right from her first invitation, Lily had loved in-line skating and sleepovers and roaming in packs of kids at the mall where she could spy on boys and run up mile-high bills on her emergency cell phone.

"Come with me to Orchard Way," Jane had implored her once.

"No way."

"Why not?"

"Because it's boring. There are no neighbors," Lily answered. "There's nothing to do. Know what I mean?"

No. Jane didn't know. She didn't understand why Lily always wanted fun and parties and people. Orchard Way had everything. But Orchard Way wasn't as fun without Lily. That was the truth. No matter how much Jane hated to admit it. That was the truth.

Lily

Morning. I groan. Wriggle my toes and fingers to get the blood flowing again. Careful not to wake Caleb, who sleeps with one arm flipped over his head and the other curled around me. His T-shirt's crinkled up around his chest. I can see his belly button, a semi-outie. I press my finger against it. Softer than the tip of his nose, but firmer than his earlobe. I can't keep my hands off Caleb. He jokes that I make him feel like a science experiment.

Sometimes it seems like I've waited my whole life to grow up and fall in love. The night of my first date with Caleb was the first time I felt completely, wholly alive. The details are as sharp as an etching in my mind. October 10, fall of my sophomore year, dry with a bite of cooling air. We took a train into downtown Providence and explored, checking out the head shops and tattoo and piercing parlors. At some point we wandered into an all-night grocery store and bought a bunch of green grapes. Each grape popped so juicy and fruity in my mouth, it was like I'd never tasted grapes before. In no time, I was drunk on them, just as surely as I was intoxicated by the grip of Caleb's fingers laced through mine when we crossed the street, or the surprising bark of his laugh, or the way the blades of his shoulders stood out like fins through his clothes. I could have told Caleb right then that night that I loved him.

Cay looks different asleep, like a marble sculpture of himself. A blue vein runs up the vertical length of his temple. I can see a scar that runs parallel to his lower lip, and another scar extending from the outer edge of his eye, Egyptian-art style. He has yet another scar in the back of his head, visible through his summer swimmer's buzz cut. Then it appears, long and pale as a shark's tooth, white-puckered and nubby to touch.

All three scars are the result of the same accident. Back in sixth grade, Caleb was attacked by a pit bull. His face caught the brunt of the violence. The dog lunged straight for it, tearing the skin from the corner of one eye and ripping the flesh from his chin. But the real damage happened when Caleb fell onto the concrete sidewalk and split open the back of his head. The surgeons had to drain the fluids from his brain to relieve pressure. For seven days, he was in a coma. He lost so much blood that Mr. and Mrs. Price had signed organ donor release forms. A chaplain was called.

I heard these snips of news because Caleb, Jane, and I all went to Peace Dale Middle Magnet School. Back then, I knew Caleb only slightly. He was in Jane's class. I was one grade lower. All I could have said about him then was that he was a sporty kid with long, gangly legs and a mean-sounding recess yell: "C'mon! I'm open, ya bum!"

When word of the dog attack got out, the whole school thrilled with rumors. From her privileged place in Miss Wrightman's class, Jane had way better information than I did. Every night at dinner, she'd give us an update.

"Caleb Price is in critical condition."

"Caleb Price is as good as dead."

"Caleb Price might pull through, but he'll be a vegetable forever."

"Caleb Price might not be a vegetable, but he'll definitely be a retard."

Each grade made Caleb a batch of get-well cards, but that wasn't enough for Jane. The facts of the accident obsessed her. How many pints of blood, how many teeth, how many days of school Caleb had lost. How many stitches had been sewn into his scalp, his lip, his chin, his eye. She began to talk about how much she missed Caleb. Telling stories about what great pals they'd been. How they'd picked each other to be lunchroom cleanup buddies. Slowly, somehow, Caleb turned into one of Jane's pretends. A character she had created for one of those games that continued to twirl endlessly inside her head.

And then one weekend Jane finagled Mom to take her to the hospital to visit the real Caleb. She got all dressed up in her best party clothes. I dragged along.

In the pediatric ward of St. Christopher's, I looked at the metal hospital cot and saw a kid whose features were too purple and swollen for me to compare them with the boy in the baggy sweatshirt who was the second-fastest runner in the school. This boy was wearing babyish, dancing bear pajamas. He was hooked up to a jungle gym of plastic cords and tubes and wires, and I could see the bag where his pee went. He was awake, though. When I stared down at him, his fury crackled back at me.

I knew exactly why. What boy would want to be spied on by two girls who'd then go give reports about his pajamas and his pee?

Jane didn't seem to get this. Or, if she did, she didn't care.

"We brought cookies," she announced, dropping the ribbon-tied bakery box on his bedside table. She leaned up on the tips of her squeaky buckle shoes. Her hands gripped the bedrail and her eyes were greedy. I could hear Mom and Mrs. Price chatting in the corner. ". . . don't mean to impose, but Jane seemed so troubled," I heard Mom say, apologetic, because Jane didn't look as troubled as she did shamelessly curious.

Caleb was glaring at Jane. From deep in his throat, he managed a throttling growl. He sounded a little like a pit bull himself. My sister was not put off that easily. She reached down and flicked the tips of her fingers across Caleb's forehead.

"Did you see that dog coming before he almost bit your face off?" she whispered, but not so quietly that the rest of us couldn't hear. "Were you scared? Did you think you might die? Did you know where you were when you were in that coma? What did you see?"

"Jane!" By now, Mom had snapped to Jane's side to drag her away. To Mrs. Price she said, "I am just so sorry!" Then back to Jane, with a shake. "I don't know what gets into you sometimes."

"Aw, that's okay." Mrs. Price looked a lot younger than Mom, and her excited, girlish voice didn't remind me of regular, Mom-aged moms, either. "Blood and guts is a natural curiosity with kids."

But Mom's hand had clamped like a clothespin around Jane's neck, ready to haul her off.

On the drive back, Jane said that when she'd touched Caleb, he hadn't felt real.

"Not human real, anyhow. More like a wet snake," she said. "Like he was breathing through all of his skin, instead of just his mouth."

"That's enough, Jane," said Mom. "Frankly, I'm pretty upset. Here you insisted over and over that you and Caleb are good friends. Then you made me drive you all the way out to the hospital. And what do you do? You try to frighten the bejesus out of him! What if you'd been the one in the hospital, Jane, and that boy had come to visit you, and he made you feel strange and scared?"

"But they say Caleb Price died and came back to life," Jane said, her voice full of wonder. "Imagine."

Imagine. Sometimes when Jane used that word, like she did now, it made me shiver. It was the same kind of shiver as when Jane told me that Major Duncan Hobhouse had lost three fingers and four toes in the Civil War. "Look at those flesh stumps," she'd whisper. *"Imagine."*

But Caleb was not somebody Jane had made up inside her head. He was for real. It scared me to think of Jane sucking him deep inside her mind and changing him.

"You don't know that kid," I said. "Not for real."

"Maybe not. But what I *do* know," and here Jane paused and looked at me, her eyes widened, "is that if you've been dead *and* alive, you're changed forever. Caleb Price is halfway human now. He's been on both sides."

"He is not halfway human!" I screeched. Jane really knew how to push me into a good screech. "I saw him with my own eyes! There's two sides to be on. The alive side or the dead side. Jane's wrong, Mom, isn't she? Isn't she?"

"Of course Caleb is one hundred percent alive, sweetie," Mom assured me. "Jane's just making up a story." Then, with a searching look in the rearview mirror, "Why do you have to act so ghoulish, Janey? I know there's a happier girl underneath those morbid thoughts."

I wasn't as sure about that.

Caleb swears he can't remember anything about our visit to St. Christopher's.

"Think, think," I'll nudge him from time to time. "Two redheaded girls? One of them in a dress and party shoes, asking you too many questions? The other one hiding in the corner, wishing she could disappear into a hole in the floor?"

"Nope, sorry. Blank," Caleb promises. "Actually, my whole accident is pretty much wiped from my brain. To tell you the truth, most of the entire year after is a haze. Doctors say it happens with head trauma."

But everyone knew that after the pit-bull incident, Caleb changed. And not just because of the constant visual reminder, since the injury to his right eye had caused permanent pigmentation damage that made it a few shades darker than the left. After his bones healed and his wounds scarred over, he slowly became another Caleb. More of a loner type, who could no longer join in for pickup games of tetherball and kickball, but instead went swimming at the Y as part of his physical therapy. The new Caleb waited for the bus with his nose deep in a copy of Thoreau's *Walden*. A gift, he told me later, from his uncle Rory. And the new Caleb had a doctor's excuse to use Peace Dale Middle's music room every morning for twenty minutes of meditation.

Sometimes I heard kids tease Caleb about it in the halls. Asking him if he could bend spoons with his eyes or where he had parked his magic carpet. Caleb never seemed bothered by it.

Indifference is weird. It makes kids think you know something they don't. When Caleb started getting his name in the newspaper for winning regional swimming events, and when he placed second playing his guitar in the eighth-grade talent show, kids, cool kids like Alex Tuzzolino, began to pay attention. Then, eventually, to reverse judgment. Deciding that maybe the new Caleb Price wasn't such a freak after all.

But Caleb still didn't care what people thought, and that only made him more mysterious. In a good way, though. Not like Jane, whose sulks and weird lies and angry outbursts had, over the years, left her quietly disliked all around.

I prop up on my elbows, lean over Caleb's face, and blow lightly. Caleb shifts his arm as his eyes flutter awake.

"Good morning." I dip to kiss him on the mouth, but he presses in his lips. "Don't worry, sir," I say in a TV detective's voice. "Your breath is safe with me. Hand it over."

But Caleb turns his face so that he's talking to the back of the couch. "You were crying last night, in your sleep."

"I was?"

"Must have been a bad dream. Don't you remember?"

I shake my head. No.

"And grinding your teeth." Caleb bares and grinds his own teeth in imitation as he glances at me. Waiting for me to say something. He shifts, picks up and twists a piece of my hair between his fingers. Red thread on a white spool.

I don't answer. I don't want to remember. I don't want to talk about it.

Caleb sighs, then swings up and stomps his feet on the floor. Cups a hand around his neck and cracks the bones awake. "I wish I could take better care of you, Lily," he says. "I wish I could make it right for you."

"Then buy me a cup of coffee at the Co-op," I answer, "because it's essential that I caffeinate in the next hour."

"That, mademoiselle, I can do."

Another thing I love about Caleb. He always knows when to back off.

Jane

Granpa could kill a bee with one finger.

His pointer finger, to be exact. As soon as the bee had landed on the hard surface of an armrest or windowsill, he'd sneak up behind it. Then, *squish* as his finger mashed its tail. Easy as pressing up a crumb from a tablecloth.

"It can't hurt you. Their stinger's up front," he'd explain.

Still. Jane didn't like it. One finger, creeping up from behind. Singling you out.

Granpa didn't kill bees for fun. He killed them for bait. "Nothing tempts a brook trout like a hooked bee skimming across the surface of the water," he'd say. "And a real bee works better'n a fake."

But wasn't a dead bee fake? Jane brooded over it. Because it was no longer real.

Inside Granpa's tackle box, dead bee husks were mixed with other crayon-bright fishing baits. Flies, these baits were called, though they weren't just flies, but all sorts of insects. Jane knew some of the names. Jeweled damsels, Cahills, peacocks, midges.

This morning, Granpa did not want to squish bees.

"Help me knot this, Janey?" he said. "You've got those skinny malinky fingers." He handed her a bead-head bird fly. It looked like an earring. A tuft of brown feather, a silver drop.

Her grandfather's hands often trembled. Jane was used to taking over the more delicate tasks for him. She liked doing it. It made her feel useful. Like clicking his seat belt into place or putting the quarters into the stamp machine at the post office. Or knotting flies.

"Might be time for us to go up to Lake Pettaquamscutt again," Granpa said.

Jane looked up. "Are you sure?"

He nodded. "Sure I'm sure."

Jane had always wanted to go back to the lake. But her first trip to Lake Pettaquamscutt had also been her last. She had been twelve. Lily had been invited, too, but she was off on one of her play dates, so she hadn't come along.

The trip had started perfectly. No matter how hard she'd tried, Jane could not find the early warning signs. The signs were always there, though. Always.

She must not have been looking hard enough.

In the car, they had listened to *Alexander of Macedon* on tape. Jane had heard the tape so many times, she knew the story of Alexander by heart. The familiar words made the car time go more easily. Her grandparents understood that.

Lake Pettaquamscutt rolled into view just as Aristotle had arrived at court to be Alexander's tutor. Two arrivals at the same time. That was a good sign.

Augusta gave her a pair of sunglasses. The sunglasses were fun. Jane pretended she was a movie star on vacation, being spied on by fans.

"Very well, then, a few autographs, and then, darlings, you must leave me in peace."

Neither of her grandparents paid her any mind when she talked out loud. Augusta sat on a blanket on the shore, knitting, while Granpa trudged out deeper into the lake in his hip waders.

Then Granpa caught a bite.

"Ho-ho!" he called. His arms jerked as the hooked fish pulled. "Here's a big boy!"

As Jane watched on in horror, Granpa came back to shore, took hold of the fish, and pounded its head against a stone. Jane watched as the fish's body jerked in a horrible death dance.

It was then that she screamed, "How could you do that, Granpa? How could you?"

"Janey, it's the only way. You need to kill it quickly. You don't want to eat him alive, do you?"

"You love fish," Augusta reminded her. "And not just trout. Salmon, tuna—"

"This is different!" Jane covered her ears and shook her head back and forth. Words felt far away and hard to get to. "It's different when you *knew* him, when you knew where he lived and his family—what if he was on his way home to his family!" Waves of sadness were crashing in her ears, over her head. She ripped off the sunglasses and threw them into the lake.

Augusta stifled a small laugh. "Oh, now, that was just silly."

But she also took the fish from Granpa, who then took Jane's hand. "Let's go for a walk."

On the walk, Granpa explained that a swift, stunning blow was the best kind of death for a fish out of water. "Because you shouldn't keep it suffering," Granpa explained. "That would be cruel."

Jane tried to be comforted. She collected some pinecones. She let Granpa wipe her tears with his yellow handkerchief.

When they got back to camp, Augusta had gutted and grilled the trout, serving it up with lemon. "Now, then," she coaxed. "Try a bite."

And Jane tried to forget that the fish in her stomach was the same as the fish in the net.

Late that night, the bad feelings came back. She imagined the pieces of chewed-up fish in the bottom of her stomach. Unchewing, reattaching, reforming. The fish hiccupped inside her. It wanted to leave to go back to the lake.

She had tried to block out the bad thought by imagining that she was lying under a tree at Orchard Way and feeling the sunshine on her skin, the way Dr. Beigeleisen had taught her.

Jane hunched her shoulders up to her ears. Flattened a hand to her stomach. She listened to her grandparents' breathing. Augusta on one side and Granpa on the other, and Jane in the middle, protected on both sides from bears. Both of her grandparents were sound asleep.

But she knew that she had to put the fish in the water. When she couldn't stand another minute, she crawled from the tent. On her hands and knees, then barefoot in the slimy, wet mud. Moving to the shore as if she were being pulled forward in an undertow.

When she kneeled down beside the lake, she could feel the fish wriggling in her throat. She leaned forward, gagging. A sour, vomity taste closed up the back of her throat.

The pain shocked her. Granpa's large hands gripped too tightly. "Janey! There you are!" His fingers hooked strong underneath Jane's armpits, rippling her from her trance as he yanked her roughly up. Her feet caught air as Granpa swung her high. He shook her so hard, she felt blood slosh under her skin.

"What are you doing so close to the water? If you're feeling sick, you wake us up! You know better than this! Are you out of your goddamn mind?"

Jane had never heard her grandfather curse. It was like

being stuck by pins. She burst into fresh tears. Then Augusta was there, her gray hair spilled loose around her shoulders, like a sweet witch, shushing her. But Augusta's heart was beating fast when she pulled Jane close, and Jane wrenched herself away.

They left the lake a little later that night. Jane pitched a fit all the way back. She tried to explain about the fish. How it spoke to her. How she had to put him back in the lake. Up in the front seat came nothing but worried silence. But the echo of Granpa's words stayed in Jane's ears. *Are you out of your goddamn mind?*

The next week, her parents took her to Dr. Fox, who worked all the way in Providence. Dr. Fox's office was more solemn than Dr. Beigeleisen's. Whereas Dr. B's office was like an art room where Jane drew pictures and solved puzzles, Dr. Fox's office was like the president's. The carpet and the drapes were so thick that they closed off sounds.

Dr. Fox was a good listener. So Jane told her things. About how she might have danced in *The Nutcracker*. About how the people she watched on television shows sometimes visited her later in her dreams. How some days everything seemed to have a secret voice–dogs and fish and even her mother's stuffed animals, who told her funny stories about when Mom was a little girl.

"My sister says I'm a liar," she admitted.

"What else does your sister say?" asked Dr. Fox.

Jane shrugged. But she pressed her knuckles to her

cheeks to hide the shame that burned there. It was terrible when Lily lectured her. As if Lily were the big sister and Jane was the baby. "She said to stop lying," Jane answered in a small voice. "She says people will think I'm strange."

"Does your sister think you're strange?"

Jane considered it. "If she did, she never used to mind. But maybe it's different now. We're older. Kids talk."

Dr. Fox wanted to see Jane twice a week. She prescribed pills to help keep the real different from the not real. "I'll see you twice a week, and the medication should even you out," Dr. Fox said. "And when you think you're ready, there's a weekly group meeting you're invited to join. To meet people like yourself, who share your challenges." *Challenges.* That was Dr. Fox's favorite word for what Jane had. There were other words. *Delusions. Paranoia. Compulsions.*

Her medications were called *antipsychotics.* Jane didn't like that word, either, and she picked off the label with her fingernail. But everyone knew what they were. The new bottles took their place next to the multivitamins on the kitchen table. In the mornings when Jane reached for them, Lily pretended not to notice. Lily never used any of the words.

After Pettaquamscutt, Augusta held Jane's hand tight at the supermarket. And Granpa stayed on Jane's side during their museum trips. His eyes were like magnets on Jane when she wandered to the gift shop or the restroom.

The next year, Granpa got sick, and then there were no more trips at all.

"We could even go fishing tomorrow if I wanted, right?" Jane asked him now as she nimbly finished knotting the bead–head bird fly.

Granpa nodded. "Oh, surely, Janey–cake. 'Course we could."

Augusta looked up. Her thoughts seemed to shift off her crossword puzzle, but she said nothing. Jane handed back the fly.

"Good work," said Granpa, holding it up for inspection. "Whoo–wee, it's getting hot." He plucked his yellow handkerchief from his pocket and mopped his forehead. "Take a plunge, why don't you? Cool off."

Jane stared at the pool. Its cold, blue water invited and reminded her. But she wasn't ready. The old frustration that had been gone since arriving at Orchard Way took hold of her, as surprising and painful as the night Granpa had grabbed her off the shore's edge. "No," she said. She shook her head. "Not yet."

Lily

Caleb drops me off at Small Farms. We plan for him to pick me up in the afternoon. I leap after the car, blowing vampy kisses as he drives away. First he'll hit his house for fresh clothes. Then he'll head to the Pool & Paddle. Since my job starts earlier and ends later, it makes sense to lend my car to Caleb.

My car. Jane's car. She never let anyone borrow it, and here I am, handing over the keys to Caleb. She'd have hated that. Mom and Dad might be kind of cranky about it, too, because of the insurance. But it's only practical. Caleb's a safe driver, so their ignorance is everyone's bliss.

The chalkboard at the checkout shack reads that I'm on shift today with Georgia Clowse and Danielle Savini. Cool. Georgia just graduated from North Peace Dale High, in Jane's and Caleb's class. As with most Peace Dale people, I've known the Clowses since I could cut teeth. Literally. Dr. Clowse is my dentist.

Danielle is from New Canaan. She's what we Peace Dalers call a summer skimmer. Her job at Small Farms' strawberry fields is purely theoretical–so that she can "learn the value of a dollar," according to her megabucks lawyer parents. In the meantime, Danielle's vacation "cottage" is twice as nice as my full–time house, and she wears a gold bracelet as thick as a bike chain. But Peace Dale kids are used to skimmers. We've grown up with their oceanfront beach pads in Narragansett Bay and their shiny convertibles parked outside the nicest shops and restaurants. To be fair, Danielle isn't totally ruined from money like other skimmers. She's fun and sweet, which is how she's blended as smoothly as a milk shake with the local circle.

Georgia and Danielle show up half an hour later in Danielle's shiny convertible, in this case a candy–apple red Ford Mustang. They're both limp with hangovers and trying to revive themselves with vats of iced coffee.

"Sorry we're late. Long night. Heller's house got wrecked," begins Georgia, yawning. "It was already wall–to–wall, and then a whole mob scene came over after the open–air TelePop concert. You know the one they had out on the bay last night? Oh my God, and these kids were so messed up, breaking their Nite Sticks in half and pouring that neon glow crap all over, like, *everything*. People had green skin, green hair." She grimaces. "Some joker even poured green on the Hellers' cat."

Danielle sighs like she wants to laugh but is too tired.

"You shoulda been there, Lily. There was more green beer than the Saint Patrick's Day parade. *So* insane. Only now I feel like death." She seems to cringe from the comment as she cuts me a look that lasts only a millisecond. But I pick up on it. Death equals Jane. And it's pretty likely that Danielle's got way too much information about my sister. Jane makes good gossip, and Danielle has enough pals here who'd be happy to give the juicy details.

The thing is, knowing about Jane and knowing Jane are two hugely disconnected things. Every day, I want to explain that to Danielle. Every day, I can't.

Instead I say, "Caleb had to work double jobs yesterday. He was too tired to go out after."

"Oh, Eeyore, it's always something." Georgia does her Pooh imitation as she waves away my excuse. Eeyore is her pet name for me for whenever I blow off stuff that seems potentially fun. "Lemme guess. The two of you stayed in and ate tofu and watched *Attack of the Giant Caterpillars* on cable."

"Something like that," I admit

"You better come out tonight." Georgia opens the register and starts to recount the bills in the till. "Alex Tuzzolino is having people over. And she's got the volleyball net set up in her pool."

"Maybe."

"Listen to her. *Maybe*. What else are you gonna do? Sit at home and sprout roots?" Georgia looks me over critically.

"Besides, I need a ride. *Somebody* can't pick me up because she's got a hot date tonight and wants her privacy."

She rolls her eyes at Danielle, who looks away, chewing at her coffee straw as she frowns out over the parking area. "This'll be an easy day," Danielle predicts, pointedly changing the subject. "Suh–low."

"No argument there," says Georgia with a sigh. "Whole month has crawled, even compared with July. Nothing you can do."

It's true. It's too hot and the fields have been picked clean. We're not pulling in even a third of the money that we did in June. Georgia says it's the natural curve of the season and who cares, anyway, since it's not like we work on commission. But I like it when there's a little more hustle.

We get down to the prep work, assembling the shallow cardboard baskets, restocking the sodas from the storage bin to the vending machine, and filling the golf cart with gas from the pump by the supply shed. Lastly, Danielle and I'll hop in the cart for that morning's sweep of the fields. Double–checking that there's no litter, no traumatizing dead voles for kids to pick up by the tail and throw at each other.

Even in the swamp heat of August, this job is pretty simple. Basic duties involve assigning pickers to different rows, tagging their empty baskets, and watching for flags. When a basket is full and ready to be brought in, the picker waves a white flag. A red flag is a call for the first aid kit.

Or, as Georgia puts it, "whine alert." More than once I've sped the cart breakneck out to the middle of the field, only to have a grouchy mom or dad ask me to take their kid back to the bathroom, or to demand stuff we don't sell, like sunblock.

Danielle and I are always field marshals. Georgia, who's finishing her fourth summer working here, is manager. She's also the one who has to take the most back talk from peeved pickers, and can do the best imitations of them later. "These aren't the ones my kids picked! Annit took all afternoon to fill this itty-bitty carton! So how 'bout I'll pay half price?"

Jane had worked at Small Farms last summer. At the end of the school year, when I was so raw with shock that I hadn't even begun to think about what I'd be doing through these months, it was Georgia who'd approached me in the lunchroom cafeteria and asked if I wanted in.

"Seeing as there's a space open," she'd explained in her plain-talking, well-meaning, Peace Dale-y way. "It might make you feel, y'know. Closer to her."

My reaction must have warned her off saying any more, but a week later I called her and took the job.

Only Georgia was wrong about one thing. Working here hasn't really made me feel closer to Jane. I hadn't felt close to my sister since we were kids, so I have no idea why I believed it would be any different now. Instead, it was Georgia I got closer to.

"You know this is my last week, Lily, don'tcha?" Georgia asks as she hands off the remaining flat stack of cardboard cartons for us to assemble. "Except for a final load of laundry and unplugging my phone, I'm packed. Five days."

My heart plonks like a stone into mud. Here it is. The first, unmistakable proof that summer is ending. Georgia is heading off to her freshman year at Northwestern University in Chicago, a city I've never seen that makes me think of blues clubs and detective agencies. Neither of which seems to jell with perky Georgia.

"Have you heard from your roommate yet?" I ask.

Georgia pauses in her carton hauling and grins. "*Finally*. She wants to color–coordinate our room, and she sent me a whole photo file of decoration ideas. It got me all revved up to get out there."

"Who'll be taking over your hours here?"

Georgia laughs. "Who cares?"

"Actually, the farm's cutting to half days by the start of next week," interrupts Danielle.

I turn. "How'd you know?"

Danielle tries to look nonchalant. "Heard it from Jonesy."

"Jonesy Small?"

"Yeah." Danielle's voice has a dare in it. Jonesy Small is the son and heir to the thirty acres of Small Farms, which also grows corn and peaches. His parents are retired to a condo way out in Jamestown, leaving Jonesy in charge. In his biweekly trips to the farm, Jonesy's relentless flirting is as pathetic as his attempts to boss us around. He isn't twenty-five years old yet, and Jonesy's already been through one marriage, one stint at Cumberland House rehab, and one night in jail after a bar fight. Jonesy's also the kind of guy who calls all females from age eight to eighty "babe." I'd heard all about him from Jane, who despised him. Georgia can do this great imitation of the way Jane used to say Jonesy's name. Half shocked and half disgusted. "Jonesy Small!"

"Why'd you just say his name like that?" Danielle glares at me.

"Because . . ." Oops. I hadn't meant to speak out loud. "Just because I'm surprised. I haven't seen Jonesy around here much."

"What if I said we went out to lunch the other day?"

"You went out to lunch with Jonesy Small?" My nose wrinkles in a reflex reaction. "Why? Did you know he used to be married?"

"Why not? Of course I know. So?"

"And he's old," I say.

"Six years' difference," retorts Danielle, "is the same age span as my parents."

"Besides, you can't count that first marriage," Georgia says. "Sasha Bell and Jonesy were high school sweethearts. Everyone said they went through with the wedding only because they're Catholics and," she drops her voice, "it was a pregnancy scare."

"Okay." I draw out the word skeptically.

"Anyway, last I checked, your boy Caleb was kind of an acquired taste." Danielle whips off this insult so fast, I'm floored. "People who live in glass houses, right?"

"Wow, hang on a minute. Caleb is my *boyfriend*," I answer, once I've taken the three seconds I need to recover. My body feels all hot with annoyance. "He's not just some last-week-of-the-last-month-of-summer fling. I mean, you can't even compare—"

"All right, folks." Georgia uses her two pointer fingers to make a mini time-out. "I think I spot a Range Rover. Prepare for the first unloading of screaming beasts."

I'm quick to give Danielle a last, vicious look, which she matches with quite a snotty little skimmer expression of her own.

"Hey. Check it out," Georgia says. She holds up a deformed strawberry, long and crooked as a chili pepper. "Poor old thing. I just found him hiding behind the register."

My heart skips a beat. Jane would have freaked. She would have believed that this strawberry was a warning. A sign of worse things to come. Stupid, of course. But Jane had always been on guard for signs and superstitions. Lord help her if her sneakers came untied more than twice in an hour. Or if she skinned her knee. Or if she was served any food that was square shaped, dill flavored, or burned. Though some warnings were more obvious. Once we had to end her birthday trip to Mystic Seaport because a bird pooped on Jane's shoulder.

"That's not a warning of bad luck," I'd tried to explain to her. "Don't you think that a bird pooping all over you *is* the bad luck?"

But Jane wouldn't listen to reason. We'd ended up having to celebrate her birthday the next week, once the whole messy incident was well behind us.

I should know better than to think "warning sign." Fighting with Danielle Savini *is* the bad luck, I remind myself. There is no such thing as a bad strawberry omen.

Still, my eyes stay with Danielle as she tosses her head and walks away from me, prepared to stick to her point and hold her grudge. My skin tingles with something that feels close to apprehension. And when nobody's looking, I can't stop myself from brushing Georgia's ugly, chili-pepper strawberry to the floor. Then I squash it flat beneath my sneaker. Just to be safe.

Jane

Her grandparents went up to the house, but Jane stayed by the pool. Lying in the grass as the hours seeped into afternoon. Gambler napped under the table, his nose twitching with dreams. The sun made lacy patterns through the tree leaves onto her skin. She watched a ladybug land and crawl from her elbow to her fingertip. A ladybug was good luck, and this ladybug had seven spots on her back. Double good.

Late afternoons at Orchard Way were Jane's favorite time of day. But they had also marked the end of the visit, when her parents started to make noises about leaving.

Where are your shoes, Jane? Go find your sister, so we can pack up.

Then Jane would have to drop whatever game she was playing, or slip out of Augusta's dress-up scarves, or find the sandals she had flipped off.

That was then.

The sun receded. Its light slanted and lengthened the

shadows. She dozed. The crunch of tires on driveway gravel startled her awake again. The car's engine sounded famil- iar. She blinked, propped herself up on an elbow.

As a matter of fact, it sounded a lot like *her* car.

Cautiously, she rolled all the way up to stand. Gambler rose and joined her, bumping along at her side as she stole across the lawn on the balls of her feet.

"Whaddaya think, Gambler?" she asked, scratching him behind an ear. "Who do you bet that is?"

But Gambler wasn't talking.

Yes. Her car. Her very own, pea-soup green VW bug had stopped right at the front door. For a single, spontaneous moment, Jane imagined that the car had driven itself to Orchard Way. To be with her.

Then she thought: *Lily.* It had to be. Lily was here.

She watched as the car's door opened. Music blared and was cut.

Then *he* stepped out, unfolding his six-foot-plus, pale noodle of a body.

Caleb Price. It took Jane a moment to register this

She watched him stretch. Back and forth, then side to side, then a toe touch. His glance swept the house before he shambled up the porch steps and flattened a hand to the front door. His other hand passed back and forth across his forehead, rubbing it like a genie's bottle. One of his habits. Jane could feel the flint of memory strike her anger. It caught and sparked inside her.

What was Caleb Price doing prowling around here?

He edged toward the living room windows, cupping his hands and mashing his face to peer through the glass. Then he stepped away toward the dining room window. Of course he couldn't see her. But the longer Jane watched him, the more she wondered what it was Caleb Price did see. Did he have the same view of Orchard Way that she did?

She turned to examine her car. Secondhand, it had been a birthday gift from her parents last year. Its hood was still marked by the patchwork of an off-colored paint job, but the car had never gleamed like it did now. Jane had preferred it dusty, broken in, with wavy traces of dried raindrops on the chrome. But Lily liked everything to shine.

Or maybe *he* was the one who kept it so clean.

Abruptly, Caleb turned from the house and jogged down the porch steps, then disappeared around back toward the barn where Granpa housed his tractor. Jane stayed where she was. She spied Ganesha, her elephant–head key–chain ornament, in the ignition.

She'd bought Ganesha at the Metropolitan Museum of Art gift shop last spring, during a school day trip to New York City. The little tag that came with him explained that, according to Hindu belief, Ganesha became the God of All Existing Things after he won a contest against Kartikay, his little brother. Jane had kept the tag in her underwear drawer and had read it until she could recite it.

When given a task to race around the universe, Ganesha did not start the race like Kartikay did, but simply walked around his father and mother as the source of all existence.

Jane had liked Ganesha because he looked like a lucky charm.

She liked him better after she learned he'd won that contest against his younger brother.

Caleb had circled around and now was back at the front of the house. At the front stairs, he reached down and pinched off a branch of verbena. It hung limp between his fingers like a cigarette as he turned and strolled down the lawn. Jane followed. Gambler, too. His tail and ears perked up taut, as though held by strings.

At the steps to the pool, Caleb peeled out of his tattered shoes and sat. He arranged himself neatly. Legs crossed, spine upright, face tipped to the sky. Jane walked to the other end of the pool where she could keep her eyes on him while also keeping her distance.

He couldn't see her. She was sure, she was positive of that. But could he see something? Caleb Price had a different awareness. Everyone knew that. Ever since that time he'd almost been killed by that dog, Caleb had lived in a cloud of rumors. Kids said crazy things about him. That he could levitate. That he was a mind reader. That his heart beat only twenty-two times per minute.

Jane had been disappointed by that hospital visit all

those years ago. She had wanted more from Caleb. She had wanted Caleb to tell her secret things, like what it felt like to be almost dead. She thought he looked so brave, with his face chewed up and his staring eyes. But he never told her anything. She'd probed him with questions and he'd glared and was silent.

When he returned to school, Caleb kept to himself. But he still didn't want to be friends with her, or tell her his secrets. She made herself forget about him.

Then he fell in love with Lily, and suddenly Caleb Price—taller, with a new, deep voice and a swimmer's wide shoulders—was a constant, bothersome presence at her house. Whenever she turned around, there he was. After school, weekends, dinnertime, all the time, too much of the time.

If anyone had bothered to ask, which nobody did, Jane would have said that Caleb annoyed her on purpose. Like at the dinner table, when he'd steal the vegetables that Jane had banished to the side—"You don't mind, do you? If you're not gonna eat 'em." And before she could answer, he'd pop a soggy floret of broccoli or brownish lettuce leaf straight into his mouth. Smiling as he chewed, while Lily giggled behind her hand.

Most of the time, though, Caleb was as private as he'd been that day in the hospital. Like the way he'd just disappear into the Calverts' walk-in linen closet, putting his hand on the doorknob and entering it like it was another room: "Hey, back in a few. I'm going to meditate."

Then twenty minutes later, out he'd come, cheerful and relaxed.

"Why the linen closet?" Jane had asked him once.

"Good energy," he'd answered.

"Caleb's read that our house was built where there used to be a Native American community," Lily had explained proudly. "He thinks the best spiritual flow is centered right under the closet."

"Probably it was a cooking area," Caleb added. "Guided by a gentle spirit, female, I think. Real nurturing."

"I've always wanted to learn how to meditate," said Jane.

"I'll teach you," said Caleb. "Anytime you want."

But *anytime* really meant *no time*. Jane knew. Caleb didn't want to spend a minute with Jane, because it would take a minute away from Lily.

She felt too stupid to remind him, so she tried to teach herself. Wedging herself in the closet with the light off, waiting for the spirit and the energy. Instead, she detected the scent of Caleb's aftershave. And then a trickle of music from Lily's room, where Caleb and Lily were pretending to do homework. Jane squeezed her eyes shut to send a message for Caleb to find her. But he did not—or would not—pick up her signals. The gentle, Native American cooking lady never showed up, either. Eventually, the linen closet became hot and stuffy and lonely, and she got out, finished with meditation for good.

Remembering this, Jane realized that she had never actually caught Caleb in the act of meditating. But she could tell that this was his plan right now. Right here by the pool. She watched. Once Caleb had picked his position, he went still. He looked asleep and awake at the same time. That didn't seem so hard. Not like something that would have taken too much time to teach her.

"Go away," Jane said out loud, breaking the silence. "This is my place. Not yours."

Caleb's eyes were almost closed. His eyelids were baby-skin thin. Dropped into the middle of her perfect day, he was as confusing as he'd ever been.

But he didn't deserve to find her, if that's what he was after.

"Go away!" She forced from each word all the meaning she could muster. Her anger was like a fiery dart shot straight from the core of her heart. "You weren't invited here!"

Now his eyes were open. Now he was looking right at her. Pinpointing her. One eye the same washed aquamarine of the pool water, the other a mottled navy, dark as a distant planet, like in those posters of Earth in her father's classroom.

But no, Jane decided. No, he couldn't see her. He couldn't have heard her, either. Impossible.

Lily

I watch the VW pull into the Small Farms parking lot. When Caleb climbs out of the car, my mind tries to snap a tourist's picture of what other people, like Danielle Savini, might see. Today Caleb's got on his washed-to-gray, below-the-knee board shorts and a bright orange T-shirt. With his black hair sticking up in uncombed points and his long limbs moon white in the summer sun, he looks part vampire, part rock star. But all I can see is a guy who is so hot that at first, I could hardly look at him without fussing with my hair or furtively rubbing on lip balm. He actually made me understand the sweaty reality behind the phrase "weak in the knees." I couldn't believe every other girl in the school didn't feel the same.

When Caleb first started dropping by the house, Mom asked me if he was on drugs. I burst out laughing.

"Caleb doesn't even wear leather," I told her. "He's the purest, most nontoxic person I've ever known."

"Oh, well. In that case." Mom took an if-you-say-so breath before she smiled.

"Finally," Georgia says, slinging her messenger bag as we start walking to meet Caleb.

"Hey, buddy." I kiss Caleb when we get close enough, and in a rush of ownership, he's my Caleb again. His lips have just enough give and just enough heat, and his hands press my shoulders with just enough weight. I try to make the kiss longer. Mint and sweetness, until Georgia hacks an exaggerated cough.

"You're late," I say, more for Georgia's benefit.

"Yeah, sorry. I had to run a couple of errands after work."

"Next time, we fine you." Georgia slingshots her hair elastic so that it bounces off Caleb's chest.

"Heya, George. Ready to roll?"

"Like you don't even know." Georgia curls her bottom lip. "I am so over this job."

"You drive," I tell him. "I'm tired."

When we get to the car, Caleb opens the passenger side door and flips the seat so that Georgia can climb into the back. I hop in front, and right away catch the scent of verbena. I lean forward for a deep lungful from the branch that Caleb has stuck in the built-in bud vase. Mmm. "My grandmother loved verbena."

Nobody answers, which makes me feel slightly dorky in front of Georgia. What is it about referring to grandparents that seems to reveal the depths of your uncoolness? Maybe because grandparents are the recipients of such overflowing doses of little-kid love, the kind of love that makes you feel almost ashamed of yourself when you get older. Like believing in Santa Claus.

Then Georgia brings up what I was hoping she'd forgotten about by now. "So can I count on you guys to pick me up tonight for Alex Tuzzolino's?"

"What's up at the Tuzzolinos'?" Caleb shoots a glance at me.

"It's her bon voyage cookout," Georgia answers when I don't. "Otherwise known as an excuse for an end-of-summer Tuzzolino blowout extravaganza." She reaches an arm in between us to switch the radio station. "Jeez, Price. Only the biggest party of the summer. You and Eeyore need to get in the loop." She makes a clucking sound.

Caleb raises an eyebrow for my answer. I shrug.

"That sounds all right," he says slowly, "and I guess I'm in, if Lily is. Didn't you say last night that you wanted to go out?" Turning to look at me deliberately. Knowing that I had and hadn't meant it.

"Yeah. Sure." I say the words like I'm reading them off a road sign up ahead.

"Like, eight-ish?" Georgia presses.

"Yeah. Sure," I repeat.

"Don't flake on me, *por favor*," Georgia warns as we turn

onto her street to drop her off. "There's five more party days left before I go away to college. My social life is in your hands."

"Five days," repeats Caleb.

Once Georgia's dropped off, I snap off the music, and the mood flattens. Usually I love these afternoons alone with Caleb, with work done and knowing that the only thing to consider is whether we should see or rent a movie. But today it's different. Alex Tuzzolino's good-bye party is like a storm front up ahead. Time feels like it's moving forward too fast, and without my permission.

"Look, if you can't hit this party tonight," Caleb says, "then that's fine by me. I'll phone Georgia. We'll watch a movie."

"No way, uh-uh." I'm a little too emphatic to hide my reluctance. "No more movies. I'm sick of staying in and watching movies. I want to go."

"For real?"

"Yep."

Caleb's smile is slow to appear, and doubtful when it does. "Well, gee, I dunno, Lily Grace. It's been a long time since we've been out. First we go to this party, and who knows what comes next? Body piercing? Drive nonstop across country? Join the circus?"

"Yeah, sure, we're a coupla nuts."

The joking is halfway to serious, though. We both know that somehow, for some reason, choosing to go to Alex

Tuzzolino's party means something deeper. It's a first step away from comfortable sameness and a plunge forward into the unknown. Just thinking about it, my insides give a flutter kick of panic. Maybe that's how changes are. Maybe the moment right before you're ready to move on is always when it's hardest to let go.

Jane

Jane set the forks and knives on either side of the bamboo place mats. Three settings. One for Granpa, one for Augusta, and one for herself.

At the kitchen counter, Augusta was slicing rounds of pink-centered roast beef. Granpa was outside on his tractor, cutting the lawn by the last light of sundown. Through the open window, the smell of shorn grass drifted in along with the faraway purr of the engine.

"Look how you've made the kitchen." Augusta smiled at her. "Gracious! Why, it hasn't looked like this since you were a tiny little girl."

"I have a good memory," said Jane. "I can fit everything back together perfectly, in my head. And now I'm going to make the best lemonade in the world."

"That sounds nice," said her grandmother. Jane loved how she'd always said that. No matter what Jane might have told her. Like when she'd announced that she was changing her name to Gwyndermere. Or that she was never cutting her hair again.

"Lily's boyfriend was here at the house today." Jane pulled the lemonade pitcher from its shelf. Out of the corners of her eyes, she stole a look at her grandmother, whose reaction was unruffled as usual. "He was driving my car."

"Lily's car, now, I'd figure," said Augusta.

"You never met Caleb," Jane continued. "Remember that story of the boy in my class who was bitten by the dog? Well, he grew up to be Lily's boyfriend. Her serious boyfriend."

"That's nice," said her grandmother.

"Lily got Caleb in the fall," said Jane, "and in the spring, I got a car. Mom and Dad wouldn't have given it to me otherwise. But you were gone, and I had nobody. It was always Lily and Caleb, Lily and Caleb. And I was left out of everything."

"There are usually reasons behind being left out," said Augusta.

This wasn't the answer Jane wanted to hear. "Lily and Caleb," she said again. "The first time Caleb came over to our house, it was like he forgot how to leave. Mom and Dad just let him stick around. They always give Lily special privileges. One time I caught Caleb and Lily taking a nap in Lily's room. Under the covers."

"If they were in Lily's room, it sounds like you were snooping." Augusta snapped two sprigs of parsley from her

window box garden and fixed one to each end of the plat-
ter of roast beef before centering it on the table.

Jane paused. The nap wasn't a good example. She
thought of how Caleb's arm folded like a wing over Lily's
shoulder when they watched television. Or how he'd pour
one glass of juice for the two of them to share. And the way
he and Lily talked, filling up the space between them with
their own language of jokes and gestures and secrets, secrets, secrets.

Augusta opened the refrigerator and handed her some
lemons. Each lemon was perfect. No mold. No squish hiding in their firmness. Jane took the cutting board down
from the rack and slid a paring knife out of the knife
holder. Augusta's lips thinned as she watched. "You know
I'd never have let you handle a knife."

"You might have," Jane said, although she doubted it.
She turned the sharp blade so that the sun bounced off its
glint.

Suddenly Augusta took the knife with one hand, catching Jane by the wrist with the other. She flattened Jane's fingers to expose the thorny scar at the base of her thumb.
"You scared me that day. Blood down your shirt. All over
the counter. The way you just looked at me, not speaking,
not even to ask for help."

Jane snatched her hand away. She remembered. It had
been the same weekend her grandfather had gone into the
hospital for the last time. Her feelings had been too big to

keep inside. She had used the knife, not to hurt herself, but to get some of the pain out.

Augusta placed the knife on the counter and crossed her arms. She looked out the open window. "When your grandfather became too weak, he left the care of the lawn to the Leonard boy, the younger one who could whistle. What was his first name?"

A little shudder tripped down Jane's spine. She picked up the knife. She remembered the blade through her skin. How it had hurt so much, and at the same time, not enough.

"Billy Leonard," she murmured.

"Billy Leonard." Augusta smiled. "I can almost see your grandfather now, on his porch rocker. How his eyes would follow Billy from every angle. Oh, and how cranky Ray'd get if it wasn't cut just so."

"He's never cranky," said Jane.

Augusta watched as Jane gripped the knife and sliced a lemon into four equal quarters. Then another. Jane squeezed each wedge to a trickle of juice into the pitcher. She added water, a tray of cracked ice, and a cup of sugar from Augusta's daisy canister. A few fresh mint leaves from the window box topped it off.

She poured herself a glass to taste. It was good. It was not the best lemonade in the world. Just lemonade. Disappointment ran through her. She had wanted to make something better than ordinary. But her perfect day was fading with the sun. It wasn't meant to last. She picked up the wooden spoon. Maybe stirring would improve it.

"I changed after your grandfather died, didn't I?" Augusta's voice caught at the end. She cleared her throat. "I didn't mean for it to happen, Jane. It hurt you. You'd come over Sundays, and I'd see your face pinched up with worries, and I knew you needed me, but I was too deep inside my own hurt. I could hardly put the coffee on, or read the paper."

"Doesn't matter." Jane shrugged, but she felt tight with the pain of remembering.

"It does matter."

Jane looked up, though she kept stirring to hear the clink–clunk of ice cubes bumping against the sides of the pitcher. Her grandmother was holding herself as still as a flagpole, her hands folded tight across her middle.

"I had a responsibility to help you." Augusta nodded. "I let you down. I'm sorry for that."

"You don't have to be sorry," said Jane. "Everything's good again." But she realized that she was stirring so hard that lemonade had dribbled over to puddle on the countertop. "You were all alone. But I didn't know what all alone felt like until you left me. Now I do. Even with you and Granpa here, I know."

They stared at each other. Augusta knew better than to hug her. Jane had never understood hugs, all that smothering closeness.

Her grandmother took the dishrag and mopped the spill. "You're here because you're holding on," she said. "You've got a grudge against the world, and that's what keeps you stuck in it. You need to let go, Jane. Your grandfather and I are just a step along the way. Don't you see that?"

And then Granpa appeared in the doorway, rosy cheeked, changed into a fresh cotton shirt and with his silver hair swept back in a puff. Jane blinked. His face was blurred. He looked like all the different ways she'd ever known him. He sniffed at the air and then, smiling, began to dance, snapping his fingers and catching Augusta by the waist as he twirled her to the tune of one of his nonsense songs. "Roast-a beef and lemon-ade and I'm a lucky man-o. Roast-a beef and lemon-ade and dancing with my girl."

As Jane watched, she could feel her grandparents lost in each other. It was the one place they created that shut her out. It reminded Jane of Lily and Caleb, and their private life together.

"Time for dinner!" she said, to interrupt them.

Augusta smiled and tweaked Granpa's nose as the dance ended. They took their places at the table. Jane could smell the tobacco and grass and cotton in her grandfather's skin, the bitter lemon in her own fingers, and the verbena that she had picked earlier and set in a glass jar, for a centerpiece. All the right smells of summer.

On impulse, she reached out and gripped one of her

grandparent's hands in each of her own, so that they made a chain around the table, the way they used to say grace.

"You see? I'm not letting go of you," she told them. "Ever."

She meant it as a happy thing, but as soon as the words were out, she knew it wasn't.

Lily

I'm doubtful about tonight, but I keep up the whole charade of preparing. So does Caleb. It's like a game of chicken. By seven-thirty, I've shaved the stubble off my legs, washed my hair, and combed it out with a daub of my new, overpriced, undersized tube of hair gloss. In my closet, I pick out my favorite dark denim mini along with an off-the-shoulder white top that I bought on sale at Wilner & Webb. The tag's still on because there hasn't been any special occasion to wear it. Till now. Maybe.

The phone rings just as I've scooted my desk chair to my closet door mirror for a long-overdue eyebrow tweeze. Behind me, Caleb bends into different angles, checking himself out. The setting sun warms the hollows in Cay's eyes and cheekbones while brightening the highlights of my hair. We smile at each other's reflections. I wish I could feel as sparkly on the inside. Just thinking of tonight dries up my mouth in anxiety.

On the second ring, I guess out loud. "La Mom." I dash for the phone, slide flopping across my bed to grab it off my bedside table. "H'lo?"

"Lily?" Mom's voice sounds a thousand miles away. "How are you? How is everything? Aunt Gwen and Uncle Dean send their love."

"Fine, fine. Everything's cool. Tell Aunt Gwen and Uncle Dean I say hi."

"And have you eaten dinner?"

"Uh–huh, those spring rolls you bought. Caleb gives them two thumbs up. He's here. We're going out a little later."

"Hi, Mrs. Calvert," Caleb calls absently.

"That'll be fun." Mom continued, "Say hi to Caleb for me."

"Is everything okay?"

"Honey, your dad and I were thinking." And now Mom *ahems.* "If you wanted to drive the car up here, both your father and I trust your highway driving enough to make the trip." There's a stamped–and–finalized way that she says this. She and Dad must have been wrangling with this topic for hours. "As long as you promise to leave before it gets too late. And not to drive in the left lane with all the crazy speed demons. Oop–hang on. Daddy wants to say something."

I hear a mumble mumble in the background. Now Dad's got the phone. "Can't you make it for the weekend, Lily? Your aunt and uncle sure would like to see you."

"Dad, I already said . . ." Then the thought strikes me—like a bolt from the blue, only this bolt is the kind that slides across a door and locks me in. Here it is, the Calvert family's new reality. This is the way it will be from now on. Now the daughter left over has to be daughter enough for two.

The thing is, I'm not sure if I'm ready to face Maine again. Last August turned out to be our last family trip, when we went up there to spend ten days at Uncle Dean and Aunt Gwen's. I hadn't wanted to go, and at first I rebelled in a passive protest, eating up all the minutes of my cell phone plan on rambling calls to Caleb, while Jane played pool and Ping-Pong tournaments with Dad and Uncle Dean, or annoyed Aunt Gwen by taking her little froufrou dog, Sartre, out on long mountain hikes that snarled his perfect doggy coiffure.

But after a couple of days, Jane and I were acting like kids again. Braiding each other's hair and making flower-chain bracelets and, in the evening, playing penny-bet poker or hearts. Or, when we felt more active, outdoor games of badminton. But those nights could get slow, too, and then I'd get antsy, throwing too much wood on the fire, or grazing for snacks in the kitchen, or reading the sexy scenes of Aunt Gwen's romance novels. Aunt Gwen said there was an ice-cream parlor in town where kids hung out, but Jane only wanted to go to the movie theater, with family.

"This is fun, isn't it?" she asked me one evening as we sat in front of the fireplace, laughing at a game.

"Sure." I'd shrugged. It was okay in a plain-vanilla, family vacation way. The fun part was how normal Jane was acting. She was always better when it was just family, who could read her moods and knew all the things not to do or say. That night, watching Jane as she slept peacefully in the twin bed next to mine, I wondered why she couldn't behave more like this in real life.

She must have wondered the same about me. Without Caleb, I probably brought back memories of the kid sister Jane had liked best, too.

But that wasn't real life. I shouldn't have to feel guilty about it.

Miraculously, a few minutes and almost a dozen good-byes and I-love-yous later, I manage to hang up the phone without having to commit to the trip.

"The parental unit is restless for a child," I inform Caleb as I roll onto my back on the bed and stretch my arms over my head. It depresses me to imagine Mom and Dad sitting out on the deck and trading upbeat comments about the view when their hearts are sick with missing Jane.

Caleb suddenly jumps over to the bed and in the next second is on top of me. "Watch out, my hair!" I squeak as the flats of his hands land on it anyway. "Ouchouchouch, Cay, get off! You're worse than a puppy!"

In response, he wriggles himself so that we're hipbone

to hipbone and toe to toe. Then he snuffles into my ear. "You smell so good, Lily–Lilliputian," he murmurs. "All cleany, shampooy, shaving creamy girlie."

"Is that right?" The edge of Caleb's nose is sharp, and his snuffling makes the hairs lift on my arms.

"Mm–hmm." Leisurely, he sniffs at my face, the underside of my chin and neck, then slowly back up to my mouth. "But ya know what else?" His voice is husky.

"What?" My giggle escapes.

"You'll never stop tasting like–sturrr–awberries!" And then he licks me, a big, slurpy, puppy–dog lick, all the way up the side of my face.

"Caleb, ugh!" But he's got me keyed up and semi-breathless, and I don't want him off me anymore. When his kisses turn serious, and soon enough they do, each one feels like it's burning a tiny scorch mark in my skin.

"But it's almost eight," I whisper eventually, reluctantly. "Georgia."

"Georgia," he whispers back, "is also known as the Peach State. The capital of Georgia is Atlanta."

"No, no kidding. We're late and we promised." I nudge him halfway off as I roll out from under him.

"Right." Caleb lets me go and sits up slowly. "We wouldn't want Georgia to miss any of her final five, fabulous party days. Geez, imagine if that was the biggest–deal thing you had to think about."

He's as jittery as I am about tonight, I guess, even if it's for different reasons. Alex's house will be packed with at least half of the nearly two hundred kids in North Peace Dale High's graduating class, all of them exploding with their plans for the future. Whoever isn't heading off to distant pockets of the country, like Georgia, will be going to either Providence Community College, Providence Tech, or Rhode Island School of Design. A full quarter of the class is enrolled in the University, where Jane had been accepted. Then there's Tamara Kerry, who is skipping school to apprentice herself to the family restaurant business, and the Giovese twins, who are giving the next three years to the Marines. Phoebe Kim is taking off to spend time with her relatives in Seoul, and Liz Joyce has already moved to New York City with dreams of becoming a stand-up comedian.

Whatever they're doing, though, everyone has a plan.

Everyone, that is, but Caleb.

But we are going. We smooth ourselves out, slip into shoes, check lights, and lock the front door. Outside, the sun is a bright pink beach ball about to slip out of a paler pink sky.

"I'm glad we're doing this," Caleb says, tossing me the keys as we approach the car.

"Why's that?"

"Been a while since I had the opportunity to watch every guy in your radius scratch their head and wonder what I've got that got me you."

"Right."

Caleb smiles as he catches me around the waist and twirls me into a clumsy dance. All spinning and no rules, the way my grandfather used to dance with my grandmother. I'd forgotten about that. I wish they'd lived to see me as in love with Caleb as they were with each other.

"Seriously. Hey, I'm not complaining. 'If Lily Calvert's dating him, he's gotta be doing something good!'"

"If you think now's when I tell you I'm the lucky one," I answer, "you're so wrong, mister."

"Ah, tell me anyway," he says. "Humor me. Tell me you're the lucky one."

I stick out my tongue. It's an old routine, where Caleb acts insecure about himself and then I'm completely unsympathetic. We haven't done it in a while, but we reclaim it as easily as a game of catch. Only it makes me wonder how much else about us we've left behind this summer.

When I open the car door, the trapped fragrance of verbena is so thick that I'm instantly light-headed. I catch my balance on the door handle. And then Jane flows back to me, repositioning herself just in that moment when she'd been farthest from my thoughts. But now here she is, smack in the center again.

Jane

The sun dropped away, her grandparents left her, and the house changed. In the twilight, it looked the way it had when Jane had seen it the last day. Back in ordinary time, with the drapes pulled shut and dust collecting in the corners. It even smelled different, of stale, unused air.

Jane moved through the rooms, frosty with the sun and life gone out of them. Gambler walked with her. His muzzle was white and his collar was frayed. He wanted to leave, too. He was finished with Jane's perfect day.

"Stay," she ordered him.

In the living room, she skated her fingers across the dust on Granpa's rolltop desk. Then she sat in Augusta's balding velveteen armchair as the twilight crept in. She remembered the last time she had visited Orchard Way. The house had sent her two signs.

On that last day, Jane had come here with her parents to help them sort through Augusta's bills and papers, and to clean up before the movers hauled off the furniture to Play It Again, a secondhand shop in New Brunswick. Lily hadn't been there, of course.

As her father had unlocked the door, a sparrow had flown in from out of nowhere, darting past them to hit a front window with a soft thud.

"Oh!" her mother had gasped. They had all watched as the stunned bird flew off in a lopsided beating of wings.

"It's gone off to die," Jane had said. "Its wing is broken."

"You don't know that," her mother had answered. "Maybe it's gone off to heal."

But Jane did know.

"Okay, folks," her father had announced as he pushed open the front door. "This is going to be a long day. We'll go at our own pace and break for lunch in, say, three hours? I think I'll start with the mail."

"Then I'll start on the kitchen." Her mother had that firm, real estate agent's look in her eye. "The fridge is probably a good attack point."

Jane hadn't volunteered to start on anything. She'd wandered out to the front hall, where her father was ripping open envelopes and skimming their contents.

"Look at this," he'd said. "Final notice, final notice, urgent. Last warning. Ma wasn't in communication with any of these companies anymore. I guess I should have figured. She could hardly concentrate on the hour in front of her after Dad passed. He meant the world to her."

And I meant the world to them, Jane had thought. But they needed to be together. They didn't mean to leave me behind.

Her second warning sign had come later, when she'd gone outside to tidy the back porch. She'd picked the crumbling leaves off Augusta's hanging plants and refilled the hummingbird feeder and then had started sweeping away the dirt. As she'd crouched to shuffle the broom along a corner, a splinter, long as an eyelash and dark as dried blood, lodged deep beneath the arch of her foot. Her scream had sent her mother racing outside.

"Good Lord, you almost gave me a heart attack!" With a hand to her heart as if to prove it. Her voice had been relieved but blaming. "It's just a *splinter*, Jane. I thought something awful had happened to you. And why are you sweeping the porch? There's loads more helpful things you can do. We need to clear out this whole house before the movers come—"

"First things first. Let me take a look at your foot, Jane." Her father had suddenly appeared, a stack of mail in his hand. "Seeing as I'm the family splinter expert." He had exchanged a private look with her mother, who had nodded and disappeared back into the kitchen.

Upstairs, in Granpa and Augusta's bathroom, Jane had sat on the toilet. Her father had kneeled before her, swabbed her foot with disinfectant, and filled a bucket with hot water for her foot to soak in. Then, using a needle and a pair of nail scissors, he'd extracted the splinter, tugging it through her skin like floss.

"A warning sign," she had said. "Like the bird."

Her father had looked perplexed. "A warning sign of what, Janey?"

She didn't know exactly, so all she had said was, "Of changes."

"Sweetheart." Her father's voice had been gentle. "Changes are going to happen whether you want them to or not. The best thing to do is to learn how to pace yourself alongside them. There's a whole life out there for you to live, and it's a heck of a lot bigger than this house." But his eyes had looked sad. Jane realized he had loved his childhood home, too. The way he'd stand in each room and breathe it in, as if he were trying to take some of it into himself.

"Maybe we could buy the house," Jane had suggested. "Then we wouldn't have to make all the changes all at once."

But her father had started shaking his head before she'd finished her sentence. Jane could see the double rolls of skin in his neck. One day, he would look a lot like Granpa. "Your mom and I don't have the money. Besides, what would we do with another house so close to our own home?"

"I could live in it."

"Instead of finishing high school? Instead of heading out

into the world and pursuing the happiness you are entitled to, courtesy of the U.S. Constitution?" He had winked.

"I *would* be happy," Jane had answered. "I hate school. I hate out in the world. I'm not the right fit for out in the world. I don't even like school spirit day. Being around other kids just makes me feel . . . more alone."

Stupid words. Her father wouldn't want to hear that. Her dad would do anything to make her happy. When she'd wanted her dream dollhouse, he'd spent a month building her one from a drawing she'd made of it. When she'd wanted to learn how to ride a bike, her dad had practiced with her until she could. And her mother was the same. It must have been exhausting for all of them, pursuing her happiness.

"You're going through a tough spell, Jane. You're a junior in high school, and you've just lost someone you love. That'd be stress enough for anyone. Don't underestimate that. Dr. Fox thinks you should step up your appointments to three times a week to get you past this transition time." He had paused, then continued, "She says you've dropped Group, too. Look, Janey, it's not mandatory, but there was a time you liked Group."

"Group is for losers." She knew it was true. A few months earlier, when Lily had caught the flu and had had to stay in bed all weekend, Jane had been delighted that she could keep Lily so entertained with stories about people in Group. People like Mrs. Samuels, who thought she was a doctor and handed everyone fake prescriptions. And Mattie Boyard, who wore weights taped to his sneakers because he thought computers were destroying the Earth's magnetic field and he was scared he'd float away.

The stories made Lily laugh hard, and that's when she'd said it, her hand coming to rest lightly on the small of Jane's back. "Oh, Janey, what a pack of losers! I don't see why you keep going to Group. You're not like them." This was true in some ways when Jane mulled it over later. She wasn't like them. Then again, Mattie's fear of drifting up to the sky felt shiveringly real when he explained it. And Mrs. Samuels had spent a lifetime in conversations with doctors and maybe her thoughts had just gotten a little bit mixed up with theirs.

"Group has been good for you, Jane," her father had continued, as if reading her thoughts. "And you have to admit that, along with the medicine, it's helped. We need to trust that it'll keep helping. Dr. Fox says it's a matter of staying with and modifying the right combination. Remember, you have a big network of people who love you." He'd squeezed her knee and stood. "What the hey. Maybe you should let your little sister give you a hand in the school spirit department. Who knows, you might learn a thing or two from her."

Jane had made her eyes go glassy-starey so that her father wouldn't think she'd been hurt. After all, he hadn't meant for it to be the worst thing he'd ever said to her.

She had decided then not to go back to Group, or to tell Dr. Fox about the warnings. During most of that fall, Dr. Fox had been advising Jane to try new things and make new friends. New, new, new. Whenever Jane listened too long, the pressure grew inside her, as if she were being over-filled with polluted water and the thinnest crack of anger would make her burst.

She had not wanted changes. And she had not wanted anyone's help in making her change, either. Especially not Lily's. Her sister hardly had time, anyway, with all her friends and clubs and everything attached to being a pop-ular sophomore at North Peace Dale High. And, of course, there was Caleb. Lily and Caleb. They hung around the house like a pair of lovebirds that could turn into a pair of hawks.

It was Lily-and-Caleb who'd reminded Jane most how it had been in the old days. Back when it was Jane-and-Lily. Her heart sank when she saw Caleb's coat hooked next to Lily's on the pegboard by the kitchen door. Her body went rigid when she heard Caleb's voice rumbling in the walls, and Lily's answering laugh that guarded a world of private jokes. He seemed to steal more room than he needed. Caleb had made the house feel crowded, and he had turned Jane into the odd one out. And with no Orchard Way to run to, she didn't know where she belonged.

Lily

"You made it!"

Alex and her boyfriend, Kevin Verdi, whoop down the Tuzzolinos' lawn to run beside the car as we pull around back of the driveway. Cars are already crammed in everywhere, and I have to squeeze for a space. Nobody misses a Tuzzolino event. It's not just because everyone knows the family, since Alex is the eighth Tuzzolino kid to graduate from Peace Dale High, with two more Tuzzolinos still to go– Tim Tuzzolino in my class and then baby sister Renee, who'll be a freshman. And it's not just because the house itself is a circus elephant of a Victorian, with four floors and six bathrooms and an all-tile pool along with a barbecue pit and a roofed gazebo. I think the main reason people congregate here is because everyone always feels so completely welcomed. There hasn't been a single time I've stopped by when there weren't at least half a dozen other people hanging out. Other towns have the local diner or pub. We have the Tuzzolinos'.

"Doth mine eyes deceive, or is it really Lily and Caleb?" Alex flattens the back of her hand to her forehead as I brake.

" 'Tis us, fair maiden," I answer. "We come in search of barbecue."

"Never thought I'd see you guys before I left." Alex looks approvingly at Georgia as we climb out of the car. "So how'd you pry them out?"

"I made them an offer they couldn't refuse," says Georgia.

"Which was?" Kevin asks.

"The joy of my company the whole way over."

Alex jabs a thumb over her shoulder. "So go spread the joy. Everyone's around back. Same old same old." She swings me into a quickie hug and plants a kiss on my ear. "Missed you," she whispers. "How're you doing?"

"Okay." I'm used to being touched in the aftermath of Jane. People want to reach out. In a small town like Peace Dale, loss belongs to the whole community. More than once it's crossed my mind how unpleasant it would have been for Jane if I'd died, and she'd been the one to be hugged and consoled. Jane, who gave birthday presents by dropping them off on the kitchen counter because she cringed from that cozy moment of thanks.

Alex is tan and strong from coaching summer–league

softball. One brown arm is draped over Kevin, who is at least half a foot shorter than she is. When they first started dating back in eighth grade, they stood eye to eye.

The height imbalance might have come as a curveball, but Kevin and Alex have the rest of their lives mapped out straight. This fall, they're both starting at Fairfield College, and they're already looking at off-campus housing for sophomore year. After they graduate, they'll have a year-long engagement followed by a wedding in the chapel at Portsmouth Abbey and a reception on the Tuzzolinos' front lawn. (I'm already invited, the band is picked, the color of the bridesmaids' dresses will be French blue.) Precisely three years from the wedding date, they'll start for kids.

At school, they got stuck with the nickname Kevex, because of the way they seemed to operate as a single unit. But it always made me itchy to hear Kevin and Alex talk about their future. Like life was just a timeline to punch in with anniversary bullets. Seeing them tonight, though, I'm envious.

"I've been dying to tell you. I got a twelve-string guitar for my birthday," Alex says shyly to Caleb. "I've had almost three months of lessons. If you promise-promise not to laugh, I want you to hear me sometime."

"Now's a good sometime," suggests Caleb.

"You're on." Alex drops her arm off Kevin's shoulder to hook Caleb by the elbow. "Do you mind?" she asks me. "I'll bring him back in a few minutes. My guitar's down in the family room. Soundproof, so nobody can hear how much I suck." She rolls out her tongue and crosses her eyes.

I don't mind. I wriggle my fingers to wave them off. But Kevin, who never has a clue what to do with himself when Alex leaves his side, gazes worshipfully after her, glances at Georgia and me, mumbles something about checking on the barbecue, and disappears.

"Um, by the way," says Georgia as we make our way toward the house, "Jonesy and Danielle might be here."

"Holy awkward, Batman." I groan.

"Maybe not," says Georgia in a way that's not really convincing to either of us.

"Why would Danielle want to bring Jonesy to a high school party?"

"Danielle's too much of a social butterfly to pass up a party. I swear she's been out every night this summer."

"So what's the deal with them?"

"Aw, Jonesy's not so bad. You were pretty harsh about him with her. There was a time when he was considered really hot."

"There was a time when dinosaurs ruled the Earth," I respond.

"C'mon, you know how this works. I stand right next to you, we play nice to Jonesy, then Caleb comes up and Danielle gets her turn to be nice. And then," she concludes, brushing her hands together, "we no longer have a situation."

"Ugh, but fine."

She smiles. "Well put."

The backyard is crowded. Kids are hanging out on the patio, by the barbecue, and in and around the Tuzzolinos' swimming pool. The volleyball net stretches across its middle. Teams are being formed. I hear familiar voices shouting familiar names. Even in the soft light of Mrs. Tuzzolino's Japanese rice–paper lanterns, the darkness makes it hard to recognize all the faces, but I wave and smile whenever my name is called. Everyone's here. All of Jane's classmates. It takes me back a little, realizing that Jane will never join in a reunion, or be noted in the North Peace Dale High alumni newsletter, or be talked about as anything but that girl who died during graduation week. I'd bet most kids know Danielle Savini better than they ever knew Jane, and Danielle doesn't even go to North Peace Dale.

I never liked the saying *Life goes on.* There's something heartless about the second, implied half of that expression. *Life goes on, even if your life doesn't.* But looking at all these kids, the truth of it hits me hard.

The Tuzzolinos have my dream kitchen. It spans a full half of their downstairs and is the beating heart of the house. The back is a lounge area furnished with plump, plaid chairs and couches plus a brick pizza oven. Tonight, the eat–in table is fully loaded with chips, dips, cookies, and soft drinks. Kids mill around it, picking and grazing, while others lounge out in front of the television.

"Lily!" Marianne Lombardo, from my class, is the first to grab me. Soon I'm hugging all the girls, while the guys hang back, acknowledging me with half waves and raised cups. It's an unexpected thrill to be surrounded by old friends, but at the same time I'm acutely aware of how separate I've been from them this summer. Thankfully, Georgia is quick to hustle me off to the buffet.

As we dig into a bowl of orange–dusted cheese chips, she nudges me. "J and D at your six o'clock. Don't look now."

I turn anyway, and see Jonesy and Danielle sharing a chair in the lounge area.

"Hi, kids!" Danielle squeals. I catch Jonesy's crawly eye, and know in a second that Danielle's tattled what I said about him earlier. His pug face tightens and he sucks in his bottom lip. Jonesy's not a big one for subtlety.

Danielle exchanges some private words with him, then slides off his lap and hops over to us.

"Poor Jonesy. It's a total kindergarten scene for him, but so what for an hour or two, right?" Now Danielle signals him over. He stands up, reluctant. "Anyway, I wanted to say bye to everyone. Hasn't this been the funnest summer ever?" This time, she doesn't realize what she's said. No widened eyes, no apologetic look thrown in my direction.

It takes Jonesy a while to cross the room on account of his ridiculous, extra–pointy–tipped cowboy boots.

"Well, well, well. If it isn't my flavey–fave strawberry shortcakes." Jonesy delivers this line with the smile of someone who thinks he's said something witty. I risk a smile back and hope it looks halfway genuine.

Danielle starts talking to Georgia about some shop in the Wakefield Mall that is selling the exact same tweed-pattern hoodie jacket Georgia has been craving, and how cute Georgia would look in it, and how maybe they should stop over tomorrow.

"Keg's outside," Jonesy mentions. "Getcha drink?"

"I'm fine." Quickly, I turn and pour myself a paper cup of grape soda from an open bottle on the table. Best to take a pass on any act of kindness from Jonesy, or he'll take it as romantic potential. After a few minutes of half-hearted listening in on Danielle and Georgia's conversation, I realize that Jonesy and I are going to have to start our own chat.

"So Jonesy," I say, "how've you been?"

"How've you been?" Jonesy re-asks.

"Okay."

"How are your folks?"

"On vacation. Visiting my mom's sister."

"Uh-huh." Jonesy dips his fingers into his back pocket and fishes out his ever-handy tin of Skol. I watch as he pops the top and prepares a plug. Then he reaches past me for a Dixie cup. His arm brushes against my boobs. Ew, how predictable. I nudge Georgia to let her know I'm finished playing nice.

"Your sister, you know. Even though she worked for me

last year . . . ?" Jonesy pauses to settle his chew into the back of one cheek. "I can't say I knew her too great."

"Mm–hmm." I watch his tongue work the tobacco into position.

"She always showed up, though."

"Mm–hmm." Was this Jonesy's idea of a eulogy? What was he not getting about my lack of desire to contribute to this topic?

"One of those chicks who kept to herself." Jonesy's forehead furrows as if in memory. "Like, not much to say to anyone."

"Mmm."

"But it was an accident, right? Isn't that the, ah, story?"

"What?" I can't believe Jonesy just said what I think he did. "What are you talking about?"

"I'm talking about how your sister died. If it was an accident."

I swallow hard. Is it my paranoia, or is it getting quieter in here? "Of course it was."

He is waiting. He wants me to tell him. He is daring me to tell him.

"She was walking across the street on Bay Avenue, in town," I recite flatly. "On the corner of Bay and Castlemark, she stepped off the curb as the light changed, and she was hit by a car. It was coming really fast, and it happened instantly, on impact. Anything else you want to know for your personal archives?" There. I'm almost proud of myself, especially that part at the end. My gaze is holding its lock on Jonesy's face, and there wasn't a single quiver in my voice to make me sound pitiful.

But then I realize it doesn't matter, because everyone who has tuned us in is watching me with sympathetic eyes anyway. Chatter continues at the edges of the kitchen, but in my immediate vicinity, nobody is even pretending not to be listening.

Jonesy raises his eyebrows. Then spits, squirting a shot of brown tobacco juice into his cup. So gross that it's sort of hypnotizing. "Huh. 'Cause what I also heard is it might have been, let's just say, not exactly an accident. The lady driving the car made a statement to the newspaper that your sister stepped off the curb and walked right in front of her car on purpose."

Suddenly I feel horribly overconscious of myself. My skin feels warm, like it's melting, as my body moisturizer turns liquid. And then the sound of my voice, thin and girly. "There'd be obvious legal reasons for her to say that," I tell him. "But if you want details about our lawsuit, sorry. I can't give out that information."

Jonesy licks his lips as if he's enjoying the anxiety of this moment.

The hush in the kitchen has gathered into full-blown silence. "Besides," I add, "why would my sister do that?"

"The million-dollar question," Jonesy drawls. "Let's just say, she wasn't any Little Miss Sunshine."

How I'd love to slap the smirk off his face. "You didn't even know Jane," I say. "Where do you come off telling me who she was or wasn't?"

"Easy, babe." Jonesy wags his head. "Let's just say—"

"Let's not. Let's not just say. Okay?" Honest to God, I want to hurt him, but my only real weapon is my cup of soda, and I have to resist an impulse to toss it in his face. Too dramatic. But without letting go of him with my eyes, I drop my arm and splash grape soda all over Jonesy's boots.

"What the . . . !" It takes him a second or so to react. Then he jumps back, scowling and furious. "What the hell'd you do that for? These are anaconda skin!"

"Oops." I replace the empty cup on the counter.

"That was an extremely dumb move." Jonesy's face is splotching with rage. "You don't even have a clue how expensive these are. But don't worry, hon. I'll be taking the bill out of your next paycheck."

"Then I guess I better quit."

"You can't quit, babe, if you're already fired." But Jonesy's bluster is getting the better of him. When he spits on the floor in front of me, some kids start snickering.

"Spittin' mad," someone says. "Watch your back." More laughter.

It's Danielle who breaks into motion first, reaching out to pull Jonesy by the arm. "Okay, let's, uh . . . c'mon."

And now I feel the shadow of a presence beside me, the quiet touch that I instinctively, gratefully, know is Caleb.

"Air," he whispers. "Breathe." His fingers belt the sides of my waist and step me backward like we're moving in a waltz, and then we turn, out of the hot light and the bright eyes of the kitchen, past the lounge and through the sliding screen doors and onto the back steps of the patio.

Outside, we collapse to sit side by side. For some reason, I'm laughing, loopy with adrenaline. "Guess I shouldn't have gone out tonight." I touch my hands to my face. My cheeks burn. "There was a warning sign, even." My breath comes in punches of air from my diaphragm. "A wise, old strawberry told me not to come here."

"Let's get you some water." Caleb stands. "Here's George. She'll sit with you." He motions to her and then vanishes back into the kitchen, as Georgia plops down next to me and bumps her knee against mine.

"So, okay, the small talk situation didn't work out exactly how I thought," she says. "*Small* talk, ha ha, get it? Pun."

"Is that what everyone thinks?" I ask. "That Jane killed herself?"

In the gap before she answers, I know at least what Georgia thinks. It's no big shock. It's not as if my parents and I haven't been grappling with it all summer. But Georgia takes care with her words as she doles them out. "Most times whenever I saw Jane in school, and this goes as far back as kindergarten, I'd think, That's a girl who just doesn't want to be here." She speaks gently, careful not to hurt. "But then last summer, when she took the job at Small Farms? I thought it might be different. Only she was exactly the same. No joking around, no stories. Jane just wasn't interested. She'd get her work done, but every day I was a little surprised she'd shown up at all. So who knows how much she wanted to be anywhere? Maybe your sister wasn't even making a choice, you know? I mean, not all decisions are like the SATs, where you get one exactly right answer and four exactly wrong ones."

I nod. We are quiet together, watching the volleyball game. It's getting rowdy. Way too many people are in the pool. Zack MacFarlane, Kyle O'Hara, Chuckie Giovese, Brian Giovese, Adrianne Dillon, Rachel Rosen, Tamara Kerry. A few Tuzzolinos, too; Brad, Tim, and Renee. Bodies sleek as pistons rise and sink as the ball sails back and forth like a bouncing moon.

Like Georgia, I've known most of these kids since preschool. I've been to their homes and their birthday parties, stood next to them in fire drills and lunch lines. This is the first night I've ever felt apart from them. This, I realize, is probably how my sister always felt.

Then Alex appears, bounding toward us from around the side of the house. "Aha!" She stops in front of me and looks me up and down, hands on her hips. "You okay? I just heard what happened in the kitchen with Jonesy."

"It was stupid." I shrug. "It was nothing."

"Usually I can keep out most of the midlife crisis crowd. But some of those geezers get past the ropes."

"It *was* kind of a bizarre experience to quit my job in front of half the senior class," I admit. "That was a first."

"Speaking of jobs," Alex ventures, "what's your boy Caleb doing, job-wise, next year? He should give guitar lessons. He's amazing."

"I know," I say. "He's seriously talented. And he's a great teacher."

"I'll be modest and pretend I didn't hear that." Over my shoulder, Caleb hands me a cup of water.

"So what is the plan, guy?" Alex asks Caleb the one question I've shied away from all summer. Funny how it sounds so innocent, coming from her.

"Dunno." Caleb reseats himself on my other side and cracks his knuckles. "I'm a work in progress."

"Hello? From the kid who's had an after-school job ever since seventh grade?" Georgia wags her head. "You're like the king of self-reliance."

Alex nods in agreement. "Yeah, I always think of you as someone who could live anywhere and do anything. Travel around from place to place, spreading the good word. Like Gandhi, or Moses."

"Or Mr. Thoreau," adds Georgia.

Embarrassed, Caleb laughs and rubs the back of his head where his scar is.

When he glances at me, the lantern light reflects in his eyes, and I can see the concern that shines in them. Concern for me. Because Alex is right, I realize. And Caleb knows it. He's not hanging around Peace Dale because he doesn't know what to do with his life. He's here because I don't know what I'd do without him. I'm the one holding him back.

How could I not have perceived for so long what must be so obvious to everybody else?

When Caleb sees my expression change, he looks away.

Alex seems to pick up on something. "Come search out Kevin with me?" she asks Georgia. "Bet you anything he went off to read his book on the toilet. He does that when he can't find me."

"That is called knowing someone way too well. You guys are such an old married couple!" Georgia jumps up. "But I can't resist. Let's sneak up on him." Laughing, they race off.

Once they're gone, I still can't get myself to ask Caleb. The words stick in my throat. *Am I the reason you're still here?* It's my million-dollar question, but I'm scared that saying anything, one single thing, will set the changes in motion. Maybe that's why I haven't spoken up before.

Then Caleb surprises me by speaking up first.

"I drove out to your grandparents' house today."

"For real?" I stare at him, confused. "How? Why'd you do that?"

"How, because you once told me where they lived. Third

left off Shaw Road. Why, I don't know. You'd always said it was the place Jane loved best. And I guess I'd been curious."

"They're going to be tearing it down," I tell him.

"Yeah, I saw the construction signs plastered outside."

This twists my heart a little, imagining that great big wrecking ball smashing into the side of Orchard Way and taking with it my best memories of my sister. I'm glad Jane will never have to see that. "What was it like?" I ask. "When you were there?"

Abruptly, Caleb slides off the step. There's an urgent pressure in his hands as he tugs me up to stand next to him. As if he's just made up his mind about something. "How about I show you instead?"

Jane

Jane left the house. Outside, the stars were a scatter of broken crystal tipped across the sky. It was beginning again. She would walk. She would become frightened, and she would start to run back. She would call for Augusta and Granpa. Pound on their door until it opened. They'd be waiting for her. She would sleep, and she would wake up into her perfect day all over again. She would eat cantaloupe and sit by the pool in the sun. Her grandmother would prepare dinner. Jane would make a pitcher of lemonade, and the sun would set, and her day would end, and her grandparents would leave, and the house would change. She would be alone with Gambler. She would leave the house. She would walk. She would become frightened and hungry and turn back, yelling, and be rescued again.

Rescued into another perfect day.

Around again around, but underneath Jane could feel

pinpricks of change. The thunderstorm. Caleb's visit. Not warning signs, no, but they made her restless.

Summer grass scratched at the bottoms of her feet. She remembered how Billy Leonard, in his frayed shorts and backward cap, used to sit on Granpa's tractor and mow the lawn during that summer he worked here. He'd let her ride with him on the tractor a few times. Billy had also taught her how to hold the mini-saw to cut away dead tree branches. How to thin, weed, and calcify Granpa's veg-etable patch so that it would bear the sweetest tomatoes and chunkiest zucchinis. Billy had loved Orchard Way. Working beside him in the sun, Jane had pretended they were New England pioneers, preparing for the winter.

At school, Billy had been different. Shy. School rules banned caps, and Billy's fizz of black hair hid the top half of his face. But whenever he'd caught sight of Jane, he'd stretch his lips into a neat line that floated somewhere close to a smile.

Yes, we have a connection, his lips had seemed to say to her.

After Augusta died, Jane wondered if someone had told Billy. Every time she saw him, she almost did. She'd imag-ine his lips pressing downward as he took in the news. Other times, she'd imagine Billy's lips pressed against hers. Warm as summer. She didn't know when she'd begun doo-dling Billy Leonard's name on her notebooks. She didn't know when she'd started thinking about Billy-and-Jane.

She'd even brought him up with Lily, knocking on her

bedroom door to ask, "Do you think Billy Leonard is ugly or what?"

"Why, you got a thing for him?" Lily's eyes had danced.

"Shut up." She'd closed the door. And that was that.

But then another time, in visual arts class, Jane had sketched a portrait in charcoals that she'd had to rip up when it turned out to look too much like Billy Leonard's wild hair and black eyes. The charcoal had stayed smudged on her fingers all day, like evidence. She imagined Billy Leonard coming over to her house. She imagined him slouched next to her as they watched TV, while Lily and Caleb had to sit on the floor because Lily was younger and it was only fair.

It had taken her a long time to approach the real Billy Leonard. Then one afternoon, she was ready. Ready *for real*. She had walked up to his locker, number 373. Waited. She'd never started a conversation with Billy Leonard before, and when she watched him strolling down the hall, getting closer and closer, she felt sick with the burden of it. The words she had practiced so hard in her head began to fade.

"Yeah?" Billy asked as he came within speaking distance.

"My grandmother died," Jane had said in a rush. "Back in September. I didn't know if you'd heard. It's why she never called you. Not because she'd hired someone else to do the lawn."

Billy's eyes had blinked rapidly. It sent a doubtful, quivery feeling through her. Up close, his face was too alive and unreadable. Not like in her imagination, or even her charcoal sketch. "Sorry to hear it," he muttered. " 'Scuse me. I gotta run to class."

"Okay." Trembling, Jane had stepped away from him. Stupid, how stupid she'd sounded! There was no such thing as Jane-and-Billy. They had not been *for real* pioneers. They had not been *for real* anything.

It was over. She had knocked on Lily's door again later. "Billy Leonard looks like a rat," she'd informed her.

"Then go get a crush on a nonrat," Lily had answered, putting down her magazine. "Or else, we could call him up for a double date. See how ratty he really is."

"What, with you and Caleb?"

"Why not?" Then Lily had taken advantage of Jane's silence by deciding to get all excited about it. She had sat up in bed and clapped her hands together. "C'mon, Jane. It'd be so much easier if you'd start out in a group."

"I don't even like him," Jane had answered sullenly. "And if I did, I wouldn't need my baby sister's help to go out with him."

"Suit yourself."

"Don't smile like that, like you're making fun of me."

"I'm not."

"You are."

"Jeez, Jane. I can't win with you." Lily had flipped open her magazine and flopped over on her side. For a moment, Jane had hesitated. No, never. Double dating with a younger sister and her boyfriend? Even if it worked, it was just too humiliating.

Billy Leonard, Billy Leonard. His name had skipped in Jane's head like a poem. It wouldn't go away. She pinched the tops of her legs whenever she caught herself thinking about him.

Dr. Fox had said that liking boys was good, a healthy thing. Part of growing up.

"But what if he doesn't like me back?" Jane had asked.

"Then he's not right for you," Dr. Fox had answered. "Everyone deserves somebody who likes them back."

And then miraculously, a week or so later, Billy had walked right up to her and asked if she'd go with him to Pizza D'Amore after school. Jane had said yes without thinking.

"We can take my new car," she suggested.

His smile appeared, a faint curve of agreement. "Okay. Cool. Meet you in the parking lot."

During the drive to Pizza D'Amore, Billy had sat in the passenger side with his hands crossed and hidden under his armpits, like he was in detention. Jane had kept watch on him. Was this normal? Did he expect her to give him swoony eyes, like those other couples she'd seen sandwiched together and tilted against their cars and lockers? Did he expect her to start kissing him right away, the way Lily kissed Caleb? Would she even want to?

At Pizza D'Amore, Billy had ordered a large pepperoni

pizza and two lime slushies, and he had paid before Jane had had time to reach for her wallet. As Billy had carried the tray of drinks and pizza to one of the red plastic booths, Jane had shuffled through her thin deck of topics. Weather? School? Except that who'd want to talk about weather or school? She had stayed quiet, tongue-tied and miserable.

It had taken forever to finish the pizza. Every silent, chew-and-swallowing moment had ticked inside her. Afterward, Billy had inclined his head toward the pool tables in the back. "Play?"

Jane nodded. Glad to stop guessing how badly the date was going.

Billy had set up the table while she'd chalked her stick, then crouched and angled for the break. Soon all Jane could hear was the crack, roll, and drop of the balls into the corner pockets. When another couple had approached them for a challenge match, she and Billy had partnered smoothly, like friends. Pioneers again.

Then Billy had said he'd better get home before his mom flipped, so Jane had offered to take him all the way to his house out in Woonsocket. Driving out farther and farther away from what she knew, she began to see the warning signs. A square, fin-tailed sports car up on blocks, a baby doll head stuck in the gutter right on Billy's street. Her pulse picked up speed. Doll heads didn't talk, she reminded herself. Square-shaped cars with fish fins might send warnings *in her mind.* That didn't mean anything *for real.*

"Well. Thanks for the ride. See ya." When Billy had opened the passenger side door to get out, he had leaned over to Jane for a kiss, and that was when she had caught sight of the pea-sized mole on his neck and the faint whiff of body odor that lurked behind his aftershave.

She had been startled by the kiss, especially when she'd felt the stab of Billy's lime-slushie-flavored tongue in her mouth, and she'd driven away upset. It wasn't the Billy Leonard kiss from her imagination. It was squirmy and wrong. Besides, didn't he know that the inside of the mouth was the dirtiest part of the human body? She had spit the kiss out the window, but part of it seemed stuck inside her mouth.

Next time, Jane had decided, she'd have to say something about no tongues.

All that next week, she'd brooded over it. It had not worked, no. It did not remind her of Lily-and-Caleb. All of her Jane-and-Billy dreams were finished, sealed with that kiss. But she had halfway hoped he might ask her to play pool again.

She had waited by his locker. When he saw her, he approached more slowly.

She had raised her chin. She could see his answer before she'd asked her question. She could see it in his walk. But she asked anyway. She had thought up the words the previous night, and she was ready to say them.

"Do you want to go play pool next Monday, and I'll drive, but I won't drive you home?"

"Listen, Jane," said Billy. "I had a good time and all last week, and I'd be on to play pool sometime. Just as long as you're cool that this is a friends–only situation."

"Friends only," Jane had agreed, relieved. "That's all I was saying. Especially with that mole on your neck, and your body odor."

Billy reacted as if she'd slapped him. Blinkity–blink went his eyes.

"Hey, what is this, third grade?" he had asked. "What's with you getting harsh with me?"

"I'm not," Jane had answered. "I'm just telling you the truth."

Only now she wondered if the truth had been helpful.

Billy looked mad. "It was your sister who asked me to take you out, okay?" Billy's chin jutted in defiance, as he thrust both hands into his jeans' pockets. "And since Lily's pretty cool, I thought you'd be all right, too."

Jane had made her eyes go glassy–starey, uncaring, but as soon as she'd returned home, she'd taken the shears out of her mother's gardening basket and run to Lily's room. In seconds, she had shredded Lily's beanbag chair. The shears had made a satisfying sound like tearing rags, with a pleasing froth of foam pellets that spilled out and scattered all over the carpet.

On the spot, Lily had confessed. "But I thought you liked him! You know you like him, Jane! I was just trying to help. To get things moving." Her eyes had been moist as she kneeled to squeeze up a handful of pellets. "Look at this, it's a total mess. You come into my room while I'm not here with a pair of shears, like a total . . . such a . . . I mean, why, Jane? Why do you have to . . . ?" She'd had to let go of the sentence. Their parents had long ago banned that category of hurtful words. *Freak. Psycho. Crazy. Mental. Spaz.* Jane could hear them in the air anyway.

"Say it, I don't care," she'd said. Then, louder, "Say it!"

Lily had bitten her lips and shaken her head.

Jane had thrown the shears on the bed. Inside, she had felt the old confusion, the feeling that she'd missed something. Because Lily was not mean, no, even if she'd bribed Billy. Lily wanted good things for her. Who was Jane supposed to be angry at, then? She itched to pick up the shears, to turn them on herself.

"Stay out of my life," she had warned instead, turning away from her sister's helpless, upset face.

Billy Leonard. Now his name jangled in her like broken music, a reminder of all the things Jane had never understood. Of all those codes that Lily had cracked so easily. And Billy's words haunted her. *Lily's pretty cool, so I thought you'd be all right.*

Everyone had always thought that at first, until they'd realized that Jane was all wrong.

Well, maybe not everyone. Her family accepted her. Or, at least, they were not preoccupied with what was wrong, the pieces of Jane that did not add up.

But family was only a tiny portion of people.

Orchard Way had disappeared from sight. In the ashy darkness, she stumbled. She could hardly see a step ahead. A soft wind hushed through her ears. She began to run.

"Augusta!" she called. "Granpa!"

And then she stopped running. The night was radiating all around her. All of the tiny signs that were not exactly warnings had brought her to this point, to this moment. Like a chain of light to guide her.

"I'm here," she said.

Lily

"When's the last time you came out here?" Caleb asks as he moves onto the exit ramp that leads to Orchard Way. The din of Alex's party lingers in my ears like a dream. I'm glad to be alone with Caleb again.

I roll my neck, stretching out the tension, as I count back. "Musta been . . . over a year ago?"

"You know when they're tearing it down?"

"Next month, my dad said. After my grandmother died, Mom listed the house with Payne–Hazard," I remembered out loud. "She did everything in her power to sell it to a nice family. For Jane's sake. She figured Jane would freak if the house was sold and then steamrolled into a car dealership or something. But nobody wanted to live in it. Mom wasn't surprised–she said you'd have to sink a fortune into updating it."

"The place probably looks pretty different now from the way you remember," Caleb says.

"Different, how?"

"Neglected."

He is warning me about something. When he turns into the driveway, which is so bumpy with rocks that it jounces me right up through my chest, I see why.

Caleb stops the car. I look through my window onto a view of overgrown grass. I wouldn't have had a clue where we were if I hadn't known beforehand. The lawn looks wild, more forest than farm country. The outline of the house doesn't form a distinct outline from the trees that surround it. I reach for the flashlight in the glove compartment.

"My grandparents took such good care of their home, I can't believe it's the same place," I say. "Jane used to call it Orchard Way. I always thought it was the wrong name, but now it seems perfect." I'm chatty to hide my nerves. "Because that's what it looks like, don't you think? All you can see are these gargantuan trees."

We get out. Caleb doesn't need a flashlight. His night vision defies human limitations. When I snap on the flashlight, its weak ray is a tiny relief. I aim the beam on Caleb's sneakers, but then detour when I see the porch steps.

"This way," he says, heading to the backyard, but I ignore him.

The porch is bare, caked in leaves and dried mud. No more flowers blooming in wicker baskets, no more mismatched porch furniture, and there's only a square imprint where the welcome mat used to be. A deadbolt rusts across the front door. Raw wooden boards have been cross-hammered over every window and stapled with NO TRESPASSING signs. Through a chink in the boards, grime has been rubbed off to clear a patch of glass.

I shine the flashlight into the living room. Four empty corners and the brick outline of a fireplace stare back. A bent wire hangs from the ceiling where the light fixture once was.

"C'mon," calls Caleb from the bottom of the steps.

I turn. "Where're we going?"

"Follow me."

So I follow, tripping down the steps and hooking my finger through his pants' belt loop so he can't go too fast. Our legs make whishing sounds through the grass.

We're heading toward the pool. When we get there, I see that it's been drained. Without water, it looks naked. I pace around it, nosing the flashlight into its depths. Dirt, sticks, and pine needles make swirling patterns along the bottom. Back when we were kids, Jane had made up a touch-the-drain game that I could never win because I was scared to be underwater for that long.

"Oh, but there's nothing down there," Jane would promise, "except for . . . maybe . . . some mermaids and . . . a couple of sea monsters. Nice sea monsters, though."

Jane was calmer than I could ever be at the prospect of friendly sea monsters. She willed me to see those things, but they lurked too far outside my comfort limits. And yet

I also tried to pull Jane into my world. But if we'd failed each other, I'd been the one to fail her first when I stopped playing those games. What else could I have done, though? I had to grow up.

Caleb sits at the deep end of the pool. I join him, slipping out of my shoes and dangling my legs over the edge. I click off the flashlight and breathe in the summer night. When he pulls an arm around my shoulder, I scoot closer. My arm circles his waist as I sink against his warmth. I ripple a finger slowly up and down his ribs, each notch distinct through his T-shirt.

"I learned to swim in this pool," I tell him. "You'd have laughed. I had all the accessories. The strap-on water wings, the goggles, the kickboard—the whole deal."

Caleb is silent. I swing my legs back and forth. My heels kick at the wall in a steady drumbeat. "I wish you'd seen the house when we were little. This was the place I remember playing—really playing with Jane."

Silence.

"Don't you hate it when people ask you what you're thinking?" I ask.

Even though it's dark, I can feel him smile. "I'm thinking that if you could say something to her, what would it be?"

"Well, I could talk forever and not run out of the things I'd want to say to her."

Caleb's hand finds mine and he binds my fingers through his. His grip is warm. "So say them."

"Now? Here?" I don't get it. "Why?"

"Why not?"

"Okay, fine. For one," I begin, mostly to humor him, "I'd tell her that I don't believe she's not with me anymore. That it's unimaginable she's not going to be maid of honor at my wedding, or a godmother to any of my kids, or sit next to me at Thanksgiving and make remarks under her breath about how someone better tell Uncle Dean not to chew with his mouth open. Remember how Jane had a thing about open-mouth chewing?"

He laughs softly. "What else?"

"I guess I'd get some of my complaints out of the way, too. I'd tell her that I'm still annoyed at those sabotage campaigns of hers."

"Sabotage?" I can feel Caleb looking at me in the dark.

"Yeah, that was how it felt. Like whenever I had friends visit, Jane'd tell them our food was poison or that our tree house was haunted. Or she'd lock herself in my room. Or she'd stuff dry cereal into the sound system. She hated guests. She hated strangers in the house. Eventually I just stopped inviting kids over. It wasn't worth the trouble."

"Huh."

"I know, I sound totally petty and selfish, right? But you asked. And that's the stuff I never was allowed to say to her. Even when we got older. You know how it was, living with Jane. All of us orbiting around her illness and never acknowledging it. We weren't supposed to make her feel like even more of a misfit. Mom and Dad and I used to go to these group support meetings, and the counselor was always going on and on about how we had to affirm Jane. Give Jane her space–or else include her, depending on her mood. To be honest, sometimes my entire relationship with Jane felt so coached, like playacting."

My heart is beating fast. I can't believe I've talked so much. But Caleb stays quiet. Listening.

"Like the Senior Dance," I blurt out. "That week just replays in my head, over and over. I can't get past it. Because it really did feel like she was off-balance. But I kept right on acting." I close my eyes. "Maybe I'd guessed, subconsciously, that she'd stopped taking her medicine. And sometimes I think–if Jane and I had ever shared an honest conversation about it before, would that have given me the courage to speak up? Could I have asked her what was going on? And maybe, if I'd confronted her, would everything be different today?"

"You can't think about it like that," Caleb says, but I know he's thinking about it like that, too.

Caleb lets go of my hand and rolls back onto the grass. I lie down next to him and wind my leg over his, hooking again at the ankle. His skin radiates warmth. My yawn feels like it stretches out of the core of my exhaustion. Caleb yawns, too, and in the next couple of minutes, his breath is even. Asleep. I don't blame him. It's late, and the grass is as soft as a mattress.

I am half asleep myself when I feel it. Same as Caleb's spiderweb. That prickle on the skin, that absolute knowledge that I am not alone.

My eyes open into darkness. "Jane," I whisper.

She's here. I could swear it. Jane is here, she sees me, she forgives me, yes, and I'll be able to find her again if I need her, yes, because somehow, inexplicably, she's right inside my reach. And yet just as I want to slip all my faith inside this moment, a moment that seems so real and strong and happy that I could grasp and hold on to it forever, the feeling is gone. Taking with it my faith that it happened at all.

Jane

Jane sat at the steps that led into the pool. The moon had turned the water silver.

She watched them as they slept.

In certain light, from certain angles, people had said that she and Lily looked alike.

"Because we're twins," Lily would say proudly, giggling at the fun of being identical to her older sister. Jane had pretended to be annoyed, but she'd secretly liked the game of it, too.

By the time Lily had joined up with her at North Peace Dale High, it was no longer fun. Jane would be walking and hear Lily's name called, and she'd dread the moment when she, Jane, had to turn around.

The kid who'd been hoping for her sister would drop back. Freeze. Mutter an apology, but Jane could always hear what their words didn't confront.

Oh. That's not the sister I wanted.

Because Lily was lovely. Lily was the sister everyone preferred. Her face was shaped like a heart, and her mouth curved up at the ends so she looked as if she were always smiling. On top of everything else, Lily had gotten all that beauty. Even Lily had seemed to know how unfair it was. From time to time, especially after the whole stupid Billy Leonard mess, she would offer to go shopping with Jane, or to play games that involved makeovers and spa treatments. Trying to tack some beauty onto Jane as if it were some misplaced ingredient.

"Let's dress up and go out tonight," she'd say. "Liz Joyce is having people over. And you can wear my new jacket that you like, the one with the inside stripe."

"But I don't want to go out," Jane would argue. "Liz Joyce is painful. She's always trying too hard to make people laugh with those horrendous comedy routines. I'd rather stay home."

"Well, you're coming out anyway." Lily would shake her head and smile determinedly. Then beg. "Aw, Jane. Please? You can't sit in your room with your sketchbook all night. I promise it'll be fun."

It was never fun.

But sometimes Lily did manage to coax Jane out to parties and concerts that she'd rather not be at. And sometimes she relented and let Lily sign her up for school committees that she didn't particularly want to join.

Other times, though, Jane wondered if she were the only

person in Peace Dale who didn't understand what it was all about. Who didn't want to go to the homecoming game, or to talk about college. Who wasn't interested in other people's spring breaks or summer plans. Those days, it felt as if the whole student body were waving from a big ship that was floating them off to their happy futures while she, Jane, bobbed alone in the ocean, forgotten.

Then she'd ask for Lily's help.

"Help you with what?" Lily was always ready to help.

Help me with everything, Jane wanted to say. Help me to be like you. "Help me find a good pair of jeans. Like the kind you wear."

And so Lily would ride along with Jane down to the flea market in Kingston to find the best pair of jeans–frayed across the front, with the ends let out–and then over to Wilner & Webb, for tatted-lace camisoles or low-rider belts or whatever Lily was convinced was the hot item of the moment. It took nothing to get Lily overexcited, hopping in and out of their dressing rooms with armfuls of clothing. "Check this! Half off! Try it on! You look great in off-the-shoulder!" Although Jane never wanted to try it on, because from the minute she got to Wilner & Webb, she was tired of useless, boring shopping and wished she were back home.

With the Senior Dance looming nearer, Lily was ready to help again. Jane was relieved. Even though she wasn't sure she wanted to go to the dance, she wasn't sure she wanted to be left out of it, either. Dr. Fox had been coaxing her to go. Her parents would worry if she didn't. Senior Dance was a big deal at North Peace Dale High.

"Caleb has this friend Greg Benson," Lily announced at the dinner table, "who wants to go to the dance with Jane, but he's too shy to ask."

"Benson of Benson's Hardware and Appliances?" asked their mother.

Lily nodded. "Yeah, Greg's Mr. Benson's son."

"So does that make him Greg Bensonson?" joked their father.

Everyone laughed too hard. Jane's stomach cramped. It was a setup, of course. She could practically hear Lily ask-ing—"Will you go the dance with my sister? You can hang out with Caleb the whole night." Probably even Dr. Fox had been in on the plan. Jane was always the last to find out. Always.

Three pairs of eyes were turned on her.

"He can ask me if he wants. I don't care."

Lily clapped her hands. "Ooh, Jane. We'll go shopping for dresses and we'll do each other's pedicures, and nobody will be able to take their eyes off us, we'll be so gorgeous!" She said it like she believed it. Jane frowned.

Caleb's friend Greg Benson had turned out to be that extra-tall-with-sideburns guy from Jane's AP Spanish class.

"He's all overgrown and weedy looking," Jane pro-nounced.

"No, he's really sweet," Lily assured her. "He's shy. You'll like him. You'll see."

"Just because you like him doesn't mean I will," Jane reminded her. "You like everybody."

Lily's smile was tight on her face. "Okay, I have an idea. Let's invite Greg and Caleb over to the house for a spaghetti dinner next week. To make sure you get along. And then you can decide if you want him to ask you or not."

"Whatever. If it's so important to you."

"Jane, it's not about me. It's about you."

"If it's about me, then cancel it. I don't want to go to the dance."

"You say that now, but you'll change your mind." Lily was used to different Janes. She went ahead with plans. On the night of the spaghetti dinner, Jane watched as her sister made a pitcher of lemonade. Then set the table with Augusta's bamboo place mats and put a vase of fresh flowers in the middle as a centerpiece.

"It looks like . . ." Jane couldn't say it.

"Granpa and Augusta's table, right?" Lily grinned. "I thought you'd like that. Now, you go ahead and get ready while I make the salad. Then I'll fix your hair. I've got an idea that I saw in a magazine. I think I can make it work."

And she did, in the form of a sleek ponytail that hung low on Jane's neck.

"You look beautiful," Lily pronounced, brushing some of her sparkle powder like fairy dust on Jane's throat and neck.

Staring at herself in their bathroom mirror, a bit of hope twitched inside her.

But once Caleb and Greg arrived, Jane knew that nothing had changed. She felt just like herself. Ponytail, fairy dust, and all. Lily had lied. Throughout the evening, Jane could feel herself shrinking. Turning small and mute and distant. Memories of her date with Billy Leonard rattled in her head, mocking her.

Finally, she stood up from the table and excused herself to the bathroom.

"You're pathetic," she whispered, scowling into the bathroom mirror. She pulled out the ponytail holder. Down the hall, she heard the sounds of Lily and Caleb and Greg laughing. Were they laughing at her? Or were they just glad that she had left the table? Why couldn't she just "be herself" the way Dr. Fox always encouraged? Why was "herself" so hard?

As it turned out, the answer was behind the mirror. Because when she opened the medicine cabinet to roll on a new coat of antiperspirant, her eyes lighted on her bottle of pills.

Of course. Her answer. She would stop taking her meds. Just for a little while, a few weeks, just to get through the end of school, the dance, and graduation.

Yes, yes, yes. How else would she find out the truth of who she really was?

The next morning was her new beginning. She reached for her bottle, uncapped it, dropped one blue pill into the toilet, and flushed. She needed to remove the evidence since her mother had been known to count pills.

"Sorry, honey," her mother would always say, only halfway apologetic if Jane caught her. "I can't stop being a mom, and your medication is very important."

For years, Jane had heard about the absolute necessity of the pills. The good they could do. It had never crossed her mind to stop taking them. Watching the pill swirl, then get gulped down by bathroom pipes, new doubts came alive in her. Would she be able to recognize herself off the meds? Would she be better or worse? Would she know the difference?

Days passed. Nothing happened. And then one afternoon, walking into the school library, Jane saw the blue sky and the budding branches of the dogwood trees through the library window. The sunlight shone onto the student trophy case. Each trophy was shiny gold like pirate's treasure. So overbright and forcefully, gorgeously sparkling that she could have burst into tears.

Instead, she glided past the library desk in mini-pirouettes, like Klara from *The Nutcracker.*

"Well. I suppose spring is in the air," Ms. Myers, the head librarian, commented when she looked up from the checkout desk. "Are you excited for graduation, Jane?"

Oh, yes. She was. Over the next few days it seemed that she became more and more excited for everything. For breakfast and for her calculus exam and especially for the Senior Dance. Even for her biweekly phone calls from sweet, solemn Greg Benson, who, as she joked to Lily, had given her a new name: "Um–um–Jane" because he was so nervous whenever he spoke to her.

Later that week, trying on dresses at the Wakefield Mall, she and Lily had twisted and twirled, unzipped and rebuttoned and decided. Silver, backless for Jane. Lilac, strapless for Lily. Kitten–heel sandals for both. They smiled at their mirror selves. Impulsively, Jane picked up Lily's hands and swung them like in the old days when they played London Bridge.

"It's going to be the best dance ever!"

"It is, isn't it?" Lily enthused.

Jane's mind hummed, imagining it all. Dancing like Klara, all the music around her and the silver swish of her dress on the floor.

But on the very next morning, driving to school, Ganesha spoke. It had been so long since Jane had heard a secret language that at first she had not understood what Ganesha was saying.

Let's get away to somewhere quiet, he suggested. *There's too much noise in my head.*

She looked down. Ganesha looked up sternly at her.

I can't now, Jane had answered in her head so that Lily, doing some last–minute homework in the passenger seat, wouldn't hear. *What about the Senior Dance?*

No, Jane. You shouldn't go to that dance, said Ganesha. *You should stay home. With your mother and your father. You already won the race against your sister, remember? You don't have anything to prove.*

You won the race, Jane reminded him. *You won the race against your brother. I haven't won anything.* In the back of her mind, she worried. A talking key chain. No. It wasn't for real. It wasn't right.

That night, she was unable to sleep. She felt dizzy. She busied herself taking old practice tests for Spanish, although she was already accepted into college and her Spanish exams were over. She took one test, then another, and another, until she had finished all eighteen tests in the book. Then, spying it hanging in her closet, she tried on her Senior Dance dress.

A nightmare stared back at her in the closet mirror. The dress didn't fit. The fabric pulled. She knew she'd gained a little weight, but the dress squeaked so tight across her hips that she doubted she'd be able to sit down in it. Worse, the silvery color made her face look gray. Sickly. What had happened? Was it a sign?

Restless, anxious, she tiptoed to the kitchen. There wasn't much to do, so she distracted herself by alphabetizing the spice rack, and then reading some of her father's old chemistry books even though they didn't make much sense. She found a pen and underlined each sentence she didn't understand, so that she could go back to it later. Then she stood with her forehead pressed against the living room window and watched, scratchy eyed, as the sun came up.

Back in her room, she fell asleep across her bed. When the alarm woke her, she saw that the ink from the pen had stained like dark blue tears down the front of the dress. She took off the dress and chucked it in the corner.

Later that morning as Jane prepared to drop her pill into the toilet, it stuck to her damp palm. She shook it. It wouldn't budge. She had to flick it off. When she licked her palm, a trace of taste remained. Bitter. The bitterness stayed in her mouth all day and seemed to taint everything that came out of it.

She started in on Lily right after school, while they were watching tennis on television. "My dress is ugly and you know it," Jane accused during the commercial. "It doesn't even have any color."

"Sure it has a color, Jane. It's silver," Lily replied. "I thought you loved it."

"Trade with me."

"I've already had my alterations. And so have you."

She's trying to make you look like a clown, Ganesha reproved from inside Jane's book bag. *Your little sister thinks you're out to steal Caleb. She wants to win everything.*

No, no. Not Ganesha. That was her own voice in her mind. A *not-real* voice in her own head, like a radio that wouldn't turn off. Jane pressed her fingers to her temples to lower the volume. "When Mom comes home from work," she said, "I'm going to get her to make you trade."

Now Lily looked worried. She primmed up her lips and didn't speak. When the commercial ended, she turned up the volume and stared straight ahead.

Jane jumped up and ran to her room. She snatched her ugly, too-small, no-color dress up from its puddle on the floor, twisting it up in her hands as she marched out to face Lily again.

"What are you doing?" Lily sucked in her breath through her teeth. "Oh my God, you ruined it!"

"You want me to be in this dress on purpose, don't you?" Jane hissed, shaking it in Lily's face. Tears stung her eyes. Nausea rolled up in waves from her stomach. "You secretly want to make everything bad for me! You tricked me! Isn't that right? Isn't it?"

"Oh, sure, Jane. That's really my mission in life. To make you unhappy." Lily had tried to sound nonchalant. But she squeezed herself into a tiny ball on the couch. As if she were the one who needed protection. Jane sat on the opposite end, the dress on her lap, picking the threads out of the hem. Lily shielded her face with one hand and said nothing.

Then Caleb arrived. His two-colored eyes seemed to take in everything all at once. He sat between them on the couch, his arm around Lily's shoulder on purpose, to spite

Jane. To show her that it was two against one. As usual. Jane picked up the remote control and changed the channel to the Spanish station.

"Is it okay to watch tennis instead, Jane?" Caleb's voice was fake respectful. Jane was sure she heard the sneering undertones.

"No, Person Who Doesn't Live Here. It's not okay."

"How about we watch your show on the commercials?" Lily suggested.

"No. I'm practicing my Spanish."

Caleb murmured something.

"What did you say?" Jane asked sharply.

"Nothing."

"I have ears. I know you said something," Jane retorted. She turned up the volume. "Now you two can talk your private, top-secret language that I don't understand, and I can listen to my Spanish that you two don't understand. Fair's fair." She sounded like a baby and she knew it.

Time to leave, Ganesha whispered from inside Jane's bag. *Let's go be alone somewhere. You're not wanted here. You never were.*

Jane stood.

Lily looked up. "Where are you going?"

"Into town, to get a new dress. A good dress. Not this trash." She glared them both down, scornful, daring them to answer back.

Lily opened her mouth, but Caleb interrupted with a quick lift of his hand.

"Okay. Sounds good," he said. "See ya later."

"Later, maybe," she answered. Her tone had been threatening, but she was uncertain about what she was threatening them with. She was dizzy with anger, but all the words she needed to express herself seemed to be packed off into unreachable parts of her brain.

She slammed out the door.

Alone, in the car, she let the tears spring to her eyes. Lily-and-Caleb. Now they were talking about her. Whisper, whisper. She'd never despised them so much as in that moment.

With her silver dress crunched in a heap beside her, she drove to the Wakefield Mall. *You and I are exactly the same,* the dress told her in a small, slithering voice, *because we are both wrong and ugly.*

"Shut up!" Jane yelled. "Shuttup, shuttup!" The dress went silent. At the next traffic light, Jane used it to wipe her sweating hands.

But even as she parked in the Wakefield Mall lot, she could feel the rage washing over her, replaced by a hot, bright dizziness. As if she'd been through an electrical storm that had her thoughts snapping like live wires. Maybe Lily hadn't been trying to trick her. And of course the dress couldn't talk! That was ridiculous. Like a story from someone in Group.

She rested her forehead on the steering wheel for a long time. She imagined going back to Orchard Way, her grandparents welcoming her inside. Augusta would take the stained dress and fold it away from sight. Granpa would tell her a funny story that would unkink the knot between her shoulder blades and make her forget about the dance. And Augusta would have ice cream, and they would all sit together, listening to the crickets.

They hadn't meant to leave her. They hadn't wanted to. It was beyond their control.

When Jane finally got out of the car, it was twilight. The smell of spring hung in the air. She slipped Ganesha deep into her bag, but she could hear him anyway. He told her to keep walking. Down Castlemark Street to the corner of Bay.

She didn't have any particular plan. There was no place that she wanted to go. She felt shapeless and fuzzy. She couldn't feel herself through her body at all. The traffic light changed from red to green. *Real* to *not real.*

She stepped off the curb. She hadn't seen the car until the last second.

The water in the pool was cold. By the third step, she was in waist deep. She kept her eyes on her sister. She realized now that she had been wrong. All of the best times that she and Lily had shared together, her best memories of Jane–and–Lily, floated back to her. It wasn't Lily's fault that she'd always had more. It wasn't Lily's fault that she hadn't been able to come to Jane's rescue, that she hadn't heard the *help me* that lived inside her head. They had lost each other equally. They'd had to grow up.

"It's not your fault," she said. "It never was."

The voice in her head was the only voice she had left, but she saw Lily's eyes open, and then she heard her sister say her name. Jane could feel her grip softening, releasing her hold on them both. She was not angry anymore. She was not scared of what came next. She was not unhappy to leave behind the faint and fading dreams of the *for reals* that might have been. She was free, and she was ready.

Gambler watched from the side of the pool. He whined faintly.

Jane closed her eyes and plunged.

Lily

Through a doze of dreams, I think I hear panting. Then my face is licked.

"Oh, nasty! Caleb!" I reach out a hand to swat him off. "Gross. I think I preferred it when you had your bad-breath phobia after all."

But when I open my eyes, I see nothing but grass, electric green in the morning sun. I lift my head. Caleb is on the other side of me. At the sound of my voice, he stirs and rolls over.

"Did you lick my face?" I ask, although now I can see that it would have been an impossible feat. I must have imagined it.

"Mmm. Do you want me to?" He moves closer, flops an arm over my hips, pulling me in.

"No, thanks. I don't think I need it." Dew has soaked through my clothes. I am totally waterlogged. How could I have slept an entire night on bare grass, with no pillow?

Not only that, but it was the deepest sleep I've had in months.

"Gee, I hope Georgia wasn't counting on a ride back," I say, remembering.

There's a moment of silence as we mull this over, and then we break up laughing.

"There's something I want you to do," I say once we're laughed out. I press myself against Cay's back. I can smell skin and sweat on his neck and T-shirt.

"What's that?"

"I want you to take my car," I say, "and go see the world."

"It's official." Caleb yawns. "You've lost your last marble."

"No, I mean it." I sit up. "Go. Leave. Hang with your uncle Rory and teach kids how to play guitar. Check out the Grand Canyon or the Great Lakes. Drive up to Canada or down to Mexico. School's over. You're free, and you've been socking away money, Caleb. I know you."

"I'm not going to leave you." He pulls one of my hands to his mouth and lightly bites the ends of my fingers. "Not till you're better."

"I don't want you to leave me," I say honestly. "You're the only perfect thing in my life. But I can't live in a cocoon, pretending that every day will be safe just because you're in it."

Caleb shakes his head, frowning. "You haven't thought this through yet. You gotta have a car for work."

"I quit my job, remember? Right before I was quote fired unquote."

The echo of a frown stays on his face, but I've caught Caleb's attention. "If I drove away to see the world, wouldn't you want to come see it with me?" he asks.

I'm silent. Leave school, get away from home. No more answering to school or parental rules. Best of all, no giving up Caleb. In other words, paradise.

I don't say a word. Instead, I stand up and toss him the keys.

It's a quiet drive until we arrive at my house. By then all I want is fifteen minutes of quality time with warm water, soap, and a toothbrush.

"I'll park your car right here and walk home," says Caleb. "And I'll come by tonight after work. Burritos okay? Or something else?"

"Burritos." He's letting me off the hook for now. Offering me one more perfect day.

He kisses me and I kiss him back, hard and quick, like a passport stamp on his mouth.

Before I lose my nerve, the first thing I do when I get in-side the house is pick up the phone and get train schedules.

And then I call Maine.

"Hello?"

"Aunt Gwen?"

"Oh, Lily!" Her voice is almost exactly like Mom's. The differences are so subtle, but at the same time so obvious, that I can always tell one sister from the other. Jane's and my voices sounded like that. Thinking that, my eyes get unexpectedly hot. I'm just touching the beginning of this, I realize. Life without Jane will be filled with these kinds of painful surprises. Life without Jane will take a lifetime to get used to.

"We'd been hoping to hear from you," Aunt Gwen is saying. "Your mom will be so thrilled. Let me put her on."

From the moment I hear my mother's voice, I know that this was the right call to make. They need me. I love them. It's that simple.

I spend the rest of the morning getting some stuff together. When I take one last trip into Jane's room, it's only to scoop her stack of clothes off the bed and put them in her drawer. Then I shut the door behind me, and I go outside to water Mom's trees.

That afternoon, I call Caleb at the Pool & Paddle. Kids are splashing in the background. "I'm on the 8:18 train tonight," I tell him. "Think you can drive me to the station after dinner?"

A pause. "You're sure you don't want to drive yourself?"

"Yeah, I'm sure."

"If your folks decide that they need that car back, you should—" but I can't make out his voice from the chaos of kids screaming in the background. "Caleb, look! Caleb, watch! See how long I stay under!"

"Talk to you later!" I yell over the noise, and hang up.

When he arrives early that evening, I'm sitting on the front step, pretending to read.

He raises the paper bag. "Still hot."

But we don't even get to the burritos. Tonight, food isn't really the priority. And even though we have the whole house, we lock ourselves in my bedroom. I want Caleb so much. I want to multiply every kiss, every second, into a thousand more. I want to keep my face buried in the warm curve between his jaw and collarbone. And I want, more than anything, to drive across the country and see the world with him.

We indulge in the fantasy, a little. Sleeping under the stars and all that stuff. It's not that far-fetched. Who's to say next summer it won't happen?

"What is it your buddy Thoreau once said, about riding waves?" I ask. "You put it in as your yearbook quote."

"Live in the present." Caleb kisses my nose. "Launch yourself on every wave." He kisses my mouth. "And find your eternity in each moment."

"Right." I like that quote. It's so Caleb. "We kinda did that this summer, don't you think?"

"I hope." His voice sounds a little scratchy, but when I look up at him, he turns his face to the wall. Caleb doesn't like to be openly emotional.

He hasn't broken off his strand of thought from earlier this afternoon. He starts up as soon as we've left the house and I'm turning out of the driveway.

"If your folks decide they need that car back, you should–"

"They'll understand everything once I explain it." I wave him off. "They'll have to understand. That's a tiny advantage mixed up in all the problems of suddenly being the only child."

"What about the insurance–?"

"Hey, Caleb," I answer, "stop worrying about everyone else except for yourself."

It's one of those rare moments when Caleb is uncertain of his next move.

So am I. All I know for sure is that a next move has to happen.

The train station is almost empty except for the bench, which holds an old man and a scraggly girl in headphones who mouths lyrics over faint, tinny music. I buy a one-way fare from the AutoTix. Caleb walks up and down the platform, along the train tracks. His fists are bunched in his pockets, jingling change. When my ticket prints, I join him.

"So this is it. Lily Calvert's dumping me." He sighs, looking down at the empty track. "Everyone'll ask what took you so long."

"You are not going to get me to feel sorry for you."

"Just joking."

"Funny, funny. So how about this–why don't you go ahead and say good–bye? Then you're the one who leaves me behind."

Caleb looks skeptical. "Are you the one joking now?"

"You don't think this is hard for me, too?" I ask. "You think I *want* to watch you drive away? Caleb, I'm hardly breathing, it hurts so bad."

He shrugs helplessly. *You and me both,* say his eyes.

"Give me a coin."

His brows quirk, but he digs a hand into his pocket. He drops a nickel into my cupped palm.

"Okay. Heads, you say good–bye to me," I tell him. "Tails, you wait for my train so that I say good–bye to you."

"We're gonna flip a coin for who gets to leave first?"

"That's right."

"You're crazy."

"Practical. Call it in the air."

When he smiles at me, though, I see everything. I see each moment Caleb and I have spent together, unfolding back to the first time he ever smiled at me. And I figure that if I can carry that smile inside me, maybe I get to keep a piece of him forever. This is what I'm going to believe. I have to.

Then I toss the coin high in the air as I listen for his call, and I brace myself for the catch.